Ben Dixon is a father of four children, teacher of French and the author behind the world of Neil Peel. He grew up in Yorkshire, grew up a bit more in Leicestershire before moving to settle in Surrey. *The Heroic Truths of Neil Peel* is his first novel. He lives in Guildford with his wife, Sarah, and children, Sophie, Isabelle, Max and Kiera.

For Sophie, Isabelle and Max.

Ben Dixon

THE HEROIC TRUTHS OF NEIL PEEL

AUSTIN MACAULEY PUBLISHERS™

LONDON · CAMBRIDGE · NEW YORK · SHARJAH

A CIP catalogue record for this title is available from the British Library.

ISBN 9781786937988 (Paperback)
ISBN 9781786938282 (ePub e-book)

www.austinmacauley.com

First Published (2020)
Austin Macauley Publishers Ltd
25 Canada Square
Canary Wharf
London
E14 5LQ

I would like to thank my children, Sophie, Isabelle and Max, for their wit and inspiration, their crazy suggestions and patience in reading the chapters. Neil and Lemony are only partly based on you!

My parents, Robin and Pat Dixon, have always supported my endeavours and believed in my creativity.

Thanks to my brother-in-law, Simon Green, for bringing my characters to life with his drawings.

My brothers, Rob and Jon Dixon, along with my best friends, Chas and Nev Last, lived many of the shenanigans in this story with me in our youth. Who'd have ever thought that such silliness would make it onto the printed page? It's hard to believe that such things happened in real life.

Rose-Anne Manning, Mark Halstead, Stephen Froggatt, Daniel Dixon and George Beevers, all read the book and provided helpful tips.

Finally, I'd like to thank my wife, Sarah, for putting up with this bonkers project.

Chapter 1
How I Became Honest

"Come on, Neil. Own up. Honesty is the best policy."

I well remember the significant words my mum said to me when I was five years old. My sister, Lemony, stood just behind her, smirking at me from underneath her straight-cut brown fringe before adopting a genuinely upset look as Mum turned to look at her.

"You can't blame Lemony when *you've* done something wrong," she continued. "You've just got to admit it."

At the time, I thought this was all rather unfair. After all, I had been happily playing with my Playmobil pirates and had set up the ship just how I liked it so that pirate Sid and his gang, the Salty Seamen, were about to board the sturdy Fishgutter. Dad had previously tried to persuade me to call Sid's gang the Salty Seadogs, but I'd explained that that would be nonsense as they were men and not dogs. He had chuckled for some reason and left me to it.

I sang to myself while playing:

One, two, three, four, five
Once I ate a fish alive
Why did you let it go?
Six, seven, eight and nine and ten
Then I let it go again
Because it bit off all my toes
Why did the fish finger?
Six, seven, eight and nine and ten.

The octopus, Inky Bubbles, was biding his time behind the rocks, ready to soak Sid's crew with his squirter before inevitably dragging pirate Barnacles away to eat for his tea. All of a sudden, a little white cotton sock appeared in my vision and punted Barnacles onto the sofa.

"Oh dear," mocked Lemony. "I think you've got a deserter."

"Hey!" I cried as I darted to fetch the prostrate Barnacles and reattach his cutlass; his grip had become a bit limp recently, and he was always in danger of letting the Seamen down by dropping his weapon at the crucial moment.

Turning back to the ocean scene, I saw Lemony tossing Sid over her shoulder towards the mantelpiece. I watched his trajectory in slow-motion; I could see that he was heading straight for the wedding photograph of Nanna and Grandad in its delicate little wooden frame. In case you're wondering, it wasn't actually slow-motion. I haven't got superpowers like that guy in *X-Men*; it just seemed like a long time.

I scrambled towards the mantelpiece, knocking the Fishgutter over in my wake but to no avail. Of course, the photograph fell, and the glass broke with a tinkle in the hearth below, just as Lemony tiptoed back up the stairs and into her bedroom.

"Neil! What was that noise?" came Mum's voice from the kitchen. You can guess what happened next, of course. Mum blamed me. I said it was Lemony. Mum called Lemony downstairs, and she appeared, looking like an angel who had descended from heaven, offering to help.

"No, Mum. I was just tidying my bedroom, and I was concentrating so hard on arranging my reading books that I didn't hear any commotion. What happened?"

Frustration mounted in me, but I fought back the tears, and instead of crying, I sat myself down facing the wall, cross-legged and arms folded with a very grumpy look on my face.

"If that's how it's going to be, then you can stay there until you're ready to tell the truth," ordered Mum. Saint Lemony even had the gall to offer help with clearing up my

pirates while Mum swept up the broken glass. I let
harrumph of disgust at how low my sister could sink.

*

I should digress and let you know that Lemony isn't
sister's real name; it's Melanie. The reason why sl
known as Lemony has become clouded over time. My m
thinks it's because she used to wear a lemon-yellow dr
when she started school. Dad thinks it's because I could
pronounce Melanie properly when I'd just started to ta.
Her best friend, Ella, thinks it's because our surname is Pe
but I find that the most fitting reason is that she's just pla
sour. She seems to take pleasure in ruining anything swee
and that's the only time the sneer disappears from her face
when she's up to mischief. More recently, since she became
an adolescent, my best friend, Stephen, has started to call her
Melon-y for two main reasons, but I try to change the
subject pretty quickly on such occasions.

*

Back to my five-year-old strop (that's the strop when I
was five rather than a strop that lasted five years; I'm
stubborn but even I may have caved in before that long). I
faced that wall for the rest of the afternoon and all evening
too. Mum had to explain what I was doing when Dad got
back from work and also when I refused to move at dinner
time. I was not going to admit to something I hadn't done,
and I accepted that I'd go to bed hungry because I also knew
that my parents would back down long before I would. Mum
even described me as "a faffing pain in the giant backside of
doom" when she thought I was out of earshot, which was as
close to swearing as I'd heard from my mother.

Just as the clock struck nine and I'd committed the exact
details of my particular patch of lounge wallpaper to long-
term memory, Dad scooped me up in his arms and carried

me upstairs to bed, whispering that we'd all forget this incident in the morning and move on.

However, I wasn't going to forget this day at all. My decision was that Mum was right about one thing; honesty is the best policy, and from that day onwards, I was going to tell the truth, regardless of the consequences.

Chapter 2
The End of Summer

Of course, I didn't bear a grudge against Mum for not believing me. After all, it was lying Lemony who had fooled her. However, I've made good on my promise for six years now and have always told the truth since that day, and my parents have come to realise that I won't lie. The truth has become instinctive to me.

Dad won't let me speak to our neighbour, Mr Bush, in case I tell him that we've been piggybacking his Wi-Fi since Dad copied his password at Christmas drinks last year. It's not that we're poor, but Dad had a comparatively humble upbringing, and he's not one to forget his roots. Also, he says that some of the nibbles the Bushes served them had Nasturtium leaves as a garnish, and anyone who gives his guests flowers to eat is a ponce and deserves whatever's coming to him.

*

August was coming to an end, and I was going to be starting at Titfield School in a week's time. Most of my friends from our village primary school, Prince Albert of Lower Piercing, were joining with me, but that was a small school, so there would be a lot of new pupils to meet. I was certainly nervous about a new beginning. My manner had been similar to many children at first, but as most others learned to use white lies to get out of uncomfortable situations or to protect friends, I continued with the truth, and my teachers had been used to me. How would new people react to my honesty? Would I be seen as cheeky, rude and impertinent while annoying my new classmates? I wanted to believe that I didn't care. I was going to be me, no matter what, and I already had enough friends who seemed to find life more entertaining with a dose of refreshing Neil Peel honesty, even if it meant getting into the odd scrape.

Stephen, Grub and I were inseparable like fish, chips and peas.

I'd wanted to call us The Spectacular Threesome, but Mum had told me that that was a bad idea, and I'd understand why when I was older. Stephen Prince lived on the same street as we did, and our dads had been friends since their school days. He had a mop of untidy ginger hair and a sense of humour that tickled me. There'd been a knock at our door at ten o'clock pretty much every morning of the summer holidays, and there was Stephen with his trusty jet-black mountain bike, ready for the day's activity. He would come inside and usually have a second breakfast, flushing scarlet if Lemony, who was now fourteen, happened to be in the kitchen at the same time, especially if she was in her little pyjamas. Stephen had definitely started to notice girls and talked about them much more than Grub or I did. He was bigger than both of us and perhaps his hormones were starting to control him more these days. At least, that's what Mum said happened to boys when they became adolescents.

On this occasion, the sky was thick with dark, threatening clouds, and so we'd decided to stay indoors until the sun broke through. Grub had arrived an hour or so after Stephen, slightly out of breath from his cycle journey; it was at least five minutes away. Grub isn't his real name; it's James, but he'd been known as Grub ever since I can remember because his surname is Grubman. He was a small, skinny, short-sighted scaredy-cat, but he was one of our own. For some reason, he was convinced that any kind of situation would result in his glasses breaking and his being left blind like Velma from Scooby-Doo. I'm not much taller than Grub, but I have more meat on my bones; I think my metabolism is a bit lazy. Lemony says that I'm a skinny kid trapped in a fat boy's body. I'm not sure exactly what she's insinuating, and she's just being mean, as usual. I like to think of myself as a regular build with blurred edges. For the past few months, I've been trying to train my thick, brown hair into a side parting, but it's resisting and tends to fall back towards a straight fringe almost immediately. However, I refuse to give up.

Grub had got a new *Dungeons and Dragons* adventure called *The Sinister Secret of Saltmarsh* for his birthday, and so poor weather provided the perfect moment for us to prepare for gameplay. Grub was going to be Dungeon Master as it was his game, so he was sitting at one end of the sofa with his legs tucked under him, biting his bottom lip in concentration while reading the thick manual to work out the perils that we'd have to face. Stephen and I were working on our character sheets, dice and pencils in hand and sharing the players' manual between us. He was going to be an Archmage as usual since he loved casting spells, and I'd opted for a Half-elf to balance our skills.

Lemony had left her pink, fluffy beanbag that we'd nicknamed Chewbacca's girlfriend in the lounge, so we were sprawled across it, lost in our nether world. Dad came in, carrying some logs in a basket.

"Morning, boys," he announced, puffing slightly at the exertion.

"Morning, Mr Peel," replied Stephen and Grub together.

"Why are you bringing the wood in already? It's still August, and it's not even cold. Do we need a fire?" I asked.

"No, but your mum says it's decorative. It's taken me forty-five minutes to stack that log delivery, and it had to be done in case the rain came. Not that there was any help from you or the women in this house. They're all for burning the bra for equality until it comes to grafting with the logs. I've put a proper shift in there. I'd have a sit down with an ale if it wasn't still morning."

Eventually, he realised what we were doing.

"Careful, team. Lifeforce low! Slaying dragons, are you? Who's winning?"

"You can't go straight into an adventure, Dad. It takes days of planning," I said without really raising my eyes away from my adventure sheet.

"Has your sister managed to drag her knuckles downstairs yet?"

"Would I be on her beanbag if she had?" I replied.

"Honestly," Dad continued, "I was never allowed to shirk chores or stay in bed until all hours when I was younger. I wish I'd been my own father."

With that, Dad left us to our forgotten realm and shuffled away to call Lemony down to breakfast, mumbling that it would be easier to raise the dead and that he wasn't Jesus Christ.

"Does Lemony have a boyfriend?" asked Stephen.

I looked at him. "Who, in his right mind, would go out with my sister?"

"Well, she *is* pretty, and she's also melon-y," he replied, raising his eyebrows.

I take back what I said about his sense of humour.

"Look, Stephen. You know her," I said. "Have you ever seen her do anything nice or heard her say anything kind? She's just not a very pleasant person."

As I was speaking, Stephen looked behind me and gulped, shuffling backwards off the bean bag towards an armchair. He looked ashen all of a sudden. I realised that Lemony must have been standing right behind me and just had time to tense my shoulders up before I felt cold water splash across the back of my head and down my back.

"Off my bean bag, bum juice boy!" snapped Lemony. "And count yourself lucky I'd drunk most of my water during the night."

I turned slowly, still hunched up, to see her sway out of the doorway, empty glass in one hand and dragging the pink, fluffy beanbag in the other.

"Daddy, can I have some money? Ella and I are going shopping, and I need to get some lunch too," she asked Dad in the hallway.

"What?" he replied. "I owe the church mouse a fiver this month. Can't you take a sandwich?"

"Oh my God!" she retorted. "Is that what you want Ella's family to think of us? Please, Daddy?"

She only ever called him Daddy when she wanted something, and he always ended up giving in to her. I waited for the only possible outcome.

"Okay. Here's twenty quid. You'll have to get a Saturday job as soon as you're old enough though."

"Thank you, Daddy!" she squeaked in an 'ickle girl' voice and ran upstairs to get dressed.

"You're not ready for someone like her," offered Grub, shaking his head at Stephen. "Perhaps I should make her a demonic character for the end of this adventure. The final boss who makes the Archmage's wand droop as he cacks himself and runs off crying."

I held out a hand for Grub to slap in collusion while wafting the back of my wet T-shirt with the other hand in a vain attempt to dry it.

We resumed our die-rolling, page-turning and fact-checking, each engrossed in our preparation. Grub seemed to be drawing a detailed map and would tell us to stop looking if our eyes seemed to be focused on him for more than a couple of seconds at a time. I ignored my wet back and took a moment to enjoy being surrounded by my friends doing something we all loved.

*

"Neil!" called Mum from the kitchen. "Will you and the boys come through for a moment? Do you remember Mrs Deanus who lives near the post office?"

"Is she the little, fat lady who still has acne even though she's in her thirties?" I called back while stacking my adventure sheets and making my way through to the kitchen with Grub and Stephen in tow.

Mum didn't answer me, and so as I rounded the kitchen door, I repeated, more loudly this time, "I said, is she the little fat lady who…"

There, right in front of me was my crestfallen mum standing next to Mrs Deanus, just as I'd described her except with her hands resting tightly clasped on her considerable tummy and her mouth cinched shut as if she were imitating a cat's rear end.

"Mrs Deanus has just popped round to introduce herself properly to you," said Mum. "She's to be your form teacher at Titfield this year. I'm sorry, Mrs Deanus. Neil has an unusual manner and sometimes says things that can be offensive because he says what he's thinking. Do you want to apologise, Neil?"

I wasn't sure how to go about an apology as I thought I'd simply told the truth. Furthermore, she was in my house. The answer in my head was that no, I didn't want to apologise, but I had to say something.

"I'm sorry for pointing out your physical flaws as you don't need me to remind you of what you already know. It's as plain as the nose on your face," I stated, trying not to focus on, or point at, a particularly large pimple on the end of her nose.

"Neil!" exclaimed Mum, exasperated as I heard a stifled chortle from Stephen and a nervous shuffle from Grub behind me.

"And I suppose you're perfect, young man?" asked Mrs Deanus.

"Oh, not at all," I replied earnestly. "My sister says I'm fat-thin and I've got a self-inflicted condition that makes me socially awkward as you can see. Lots of people don't like me because of it, and I'm pretty nervous about starting at Titfield in case it gets me into bother with the other boys and girls, or the teachers too for that matter. I'm very glad to have met you before next week so that you might understand in case I put my foot in it."

"I have read the reference that Prince Albert sent across, and that's really why I wanted to meet you," continued Mrs

Deanus, softening her expression. "I'm not going round to see all of the new pupils, you know. It did say that you have good intentions, and that you aren't a mean boy, but perhaps you can work on saying nothing if there's a time when you think you might create a scene."

"I'll definitely try," I said. "In fact, I wouldn't have said you were fat and had acne if I'd known you were here."

"Quite," said Mrs Deanus as Dad came in through the back door, wiping his feet and looking at our guest.

"John, this is Mrs Deanus. She's to be Neil's form teacher at Titfield this year," announced Mum.

"Oooh. Good luck with that," said Dad jovially, while shaking Mrs Deanus by the hand. "You should be aware that he sometimes says…"

"I am aware, and he already has," interrupted Mrs Deanus, heading towards the door.

"Oh. Sorry about that. Too much information dot com," said Dad, cringing.

We said our goodbyes, and Mum watched Mrs Deanus waddle away from our house before rolling her eyes as Grub, Stephen and I headed back to the lounge.

"Mate, I can't believe you just said that!" cried Stephen, putting his hand across my shoulders.

"I hope she doesn't hate us for the whole year," added Grub before his serious expression melted away into a smirk that made me smile, and suddenly, we were all three laughing heartily.

Once our mirth had subsided, we turned back to our game sheets, but I heard Mum laughing hysterically in the kitchen too. Perhaps Dad had told her a joke.

Chapter 3
A New Term Starts

Of course, summers can't last forever, and the last few days of the holidays rapidly disappeared as I anxiously awaited my new start at Titfield. I didn't sleep as well as usual, and I'd spend time opening my wardrobe to look through the brand-new uniform that I would soon be wearing every day. I liked the smell of the new clothes, and the colours weren't that bad either. Grey trousers and a white shirt were standard, along with the purple and blue striped tie. The blazer was a dark burgundy with the school crest of a portcullis on the pocket. To me, that looked a little like a prison, but I tried to dismiss that thought and hope for the best. My friend Matthew, who was at Prince Albert with me but was now going to the private school in Lowcester, was the same age as me, and he was going to have to wear a bright orange blazer and cap for his school. Worse still, he would have to walk through the town centre to catch his bus. Savage.

I'd seen Grub and Stephen most of the last few days, and we'd more often than not cycled down to our favourite spot by the stream which was quite wide but nowhere near big enough to be called a river. It flowed around Lower Piercing, and we'd followed it as far as a tree whose limbs stretched out over the stream like sinister fingers, almost to the other side. This must have been a popular spot in the past as someone had hung a rope around one of the branches, and you could swing out in a wide arc before landing safely—if you got it right. Thankfully, there was a large knot tied in the bottom of the rope, so you could clasp your thighs around and sit on the knot. Occasionally, however, if you timed your jump wrongly, the rope would catch on what we called 'the notch' and then it would jolt suddenly, squashing your pods. It had happened to us all, but it was worth the risk as the sensation of swinging all the way around was exhilarating, especially if you managed a skilful dismount.

I should probably say that although I enjoyed cycling and mucking around with my friends in a semi-active way, I despised all team sports, and that was another thing that concerned me about starting at Titfield. I've never been co-ordinated with a ball at my feet, in my hands or on the end of a stick, bat or racquet, and the competitive gene seems to be missing from my make-up. I saw PE lessons as a way to have fun, but there could well be sports fixtures at Titfield, and winning or losing may be important to them; making excuses and getting out of things isn't easy when you always tell the truth.

Nerves aside, I suppose I was quite excited about starting a new chapter too, especially as I'd now met Mrs Deanus, and she would at least be a familiar face.

I woke up very early on the first day, beating my alarm by a full hour. I'd already set out my uniform on the chair by my bed and pulled on each item of clothing with reverence. I'd even got new pants, age 11–12, as Mum had thought that I might have to get changed for swimming or PE in front of the others and that my age 7–9 Super Mario favourites were perhaps not appropriate anymore, even though they still fitted me just fine. I combed my thick brown hair into its side parting and put some water on the bit at the back that always stuck up from the way I'd slept; I felt that I looked very smart indeed.

Dawn had just about broken as I went downstairs to get my breakfast, and Mum must have heard me opening or closing my bedroom door as she appeared in the kitchen, yawning, pulling on her dressing gown and smoothing down her wavy, auburn hair.

"Why are you up so early, sweetheart? Can't you sleep?" she asked as she snaked an arm around my shoulders to give me a tired hug and a kiss on the top of my head.

"I suppose I'm a bit excited and a bit nervous," I replied shaking my cereal into a bowl, "and I don't want to miss the bus on my first day."

"The bus doesn't go until eight o'clock, and it's only just after quarter past six," assured Mum, yawning again and turning it into a kind of 'oi, oi, oi' sound. "By the way, be careful with the milk. You don't want to spill it down your new…"

I looked down at my milk-splattered, brand new shirt and turned to go upstairs to change it.

"Hang on," called Mum. "You may as well eat breakfast in that one and then change, just in case you spill on the fresh one too."

"Good idea," I murmured, just as a bran flake tumbled from my lip onto my chest. I smiled at Mum who rolled her eyes and suggested that perhaps I should have breakfast in my pyjamas in future and get changed afterwards. This did not seem like a bad idea.

*

The times that Mum and Dad had to arrive at work meant that they couldn't drive us to school, so we were catching the bus. That was fine by me because Stephen and Grub were also taking the same bus, so we could all go in together. Mum had tried to ask Lemony to watch out for me on my first day, but she had barely even replied. Since she wasn't ready anyway, I left the house before her and knocked for Stephen on the way through to the bus stop on Gooch Street, Lower Piercing. We arrived with a good twenty minutes to spare, and Grub arrived soon after us. I think Grub's parents had bought him a uniform to grow into, as he kept having to hitch up his trousers to avoid walking on them and pull back his jacket sleeves if he wanted to do anything with his hands.

It was to be expected that we were all nervous, but something else seemed to be bothering Stephen that morning.

"What's up with you?" I asked. "You don't need to be that bothered. We're all in the same class after all."

"It's not that," he replied in a hushed tone. "Because I got up earlier than usual this morning, I went into the bathroom and saw my mum naked. She hadn't locked the door, and I saw *everything*. I'm not sure how to talk to her this afternoon when I get back home. It'll be weird."

"Gross!" replied Grub. "My mum would never let that happen. She'd lock the bathroom door twice, even if there was nobody else in the house."

I thought about the time that my mum had gone topless on a beach in Mykonos about five years ago. I think that was the last time I'd seen her boobs, but I certainly hadn't seen her fully naked in ages. Plus, this sort of thing was different when you're eleven. I could understand why that was troubling Stephen.

"You'll soon forget it when we get to school, and just don't mention it when you get home. Act normal, and it'll all go away soon enough. You should also probably knock before going into the bathroom in future," I said reassuringly.

As we were chatting, various other children started arriving. There was a particularly plump boy with a basin haircut whose equally plump parents had accompanied him to the bus stop. His mother was dabbing tears from her eyes with a delicate handkerchief while saying goodbye. Her husband handed the boy a substantial bag with his lunch inside before turning to guide the sobbing mother away. She managed to walk twenty yards before turning to exclaim, "Good luck, Wilberforce! We love you!"

"Tough," muttered Grub, shoving his hands in his pockets and hoisting his trousers up.

Wilberforce didn't seem unduly embarrassed, however, and stuffed his hand into his lunch bag, pulling out a Danish pastry.

A pair of girls that I didn't recognise arrived together, also in brand new uniform; they must have been from the other Lower Piercing primary school, Princess Albertina.

"Oi! Lard-ass!" came a sudden cry from our left.

A scruffy-looking, long-nosed boy with his peanut-knotted tie pulled way down strode confidently towards us with a terrier-like, smaller boy trotting next to him. I recognised the obvious minion as Batesy, who had been at Prince Albert with us. He was an annoying, weasel-faced toe-rag who had been boasting before we broke up for summer that his best friend, 'Basher' Walker would be joining Titfield in September, so we had better show respect.

They strode past us and made straight for Wilberforce who was still chewing a mouthful of his Danish pastry.

"Yeah, lard-ass!" echoed Batesy with a high-pitched snigger.

"What you got in that bag, fatty?" threatened Walker, grabbing Wilberforce by the scruff of his shirt.

"Can we do 'im Basher? Let's duff 'im in!" exclaimed Batesy, hopping with excitement.

Spluttering through puff pastry crumbs and custard, Wilberforce pronounced something like "Blurgle! Shreeble! Please spare me, bully!" He was blinking, his eyes wide in terror, and he had dropped his bag, holding up his hands in surrender.

There was quite a crowd now, and we were right next to the scene, so I bent over and picked up Wilberforce's lunch bag. Walker snapped his gaze around to me as he slowly released the quaking Wilberforce from his grasp.

"And who asked you to interfere, Fat Gollum?" he said, eyeballing me now. "This isn't any of your bizzle, do you know what I mean?"

Taking him literally, I answered, "No. I don't know what you mean. I'm not sure what 'bizzle' is."

"Well, perhaps you're about to find out. You've just made a schoolboy error," said Walker, turning to square up to me.

"But I am a schoolboy," I answered, stepping backwards. "I'm not likely to make grown-up errors."

I'd hoped that Stephen and Grub would have appeared at my sides in solidarity; well, at least Stephen, as Grub would have avoided any sort of conflict and let me take a beating if it meant his glasses would have remained intact. I was beginning to fear that I'd need a third shirt today, milk spilt on the first one and now, possibly, blood on the second. I prepared my belly for a thump and also tensed up to avoid wetting myself with fear. I was now at the centre of an unpleasant scene, and I hadn't even got through the school gates yet.

My salvation came not from one of my friends but from a quiet voice on my right.

"Give it a rest, Walker. It's the first day."

"Well, well. Another country heard from," spat Walker as he glanced away from me towards the origin of the voice. A boy with short, mousy, curly hair stepped forwards calmly, took the lunch bag from me and handed it to Wilberforce.

"It isn't yours," he muttered, fixing the bully with a glassy stare, undeterred that Walker was almost a head taller than him.

I noticed that Walker's knotted features had softened somewhat. These two obviously knew each other, and Walker was in danger of losing face. There was a great deal of tension as Walker clenched a fist at his side. Batesy looked from his hero to this obstacle and back again. Neither one moved nor spoke until, finally, the bus drew up to the kerb, the noise of squeaking brakes and the rush of air as the doors opened, distracting us all. There were audible sighs of relief as Walker and Batesy broke away and pushed to the front of the queue in order to be first on board to command the back seat.

I spotted Lemony who must have arrived during the confrontation. She was chatting with her friend Ella and didn't even look my way as she pushed by me to get on board.

"Thanks, Cameron," said Wilberforce, stuffing his lunch bag into his school bag. "I thought I was done for." The boy nodded and then stood aside to let other pupils get on the bus before him.

Wilberforce thanked me too for intervening on his behalf, so we asked who Cameron was.

"Cameron Dufresne," said Wilberforce. "We were all at Princess Albertina together. He was the only one who Basher Walker didn't bully. Nobody knows why. He's not particularly clever or sporty, and he keeps mostly to himself, but he's really confident, and he seems to be like kryptonite for Walker."

We found our places, four and five rows back on the right-hand side; far enough away from Walker at the back but not right at the front. I sat next to Stephen, and Grub sat by Wilberforce as he was skinny enough to need less room, space that Wilberforce required. Cameron got on last and came and sat by the window in the seats opposite Stephen and me. He spent the whole journey looking out of the window with a half-smile on his face. He didn't talk to anyone, and he just seemed more mature than anybody else, as if he was an adult in a child's body, someone who had worked out that you really didn't need to sweat the small stuff.

I could see why some people might have thought he was strange. He had a quiet manner about him, a way of walking and talking that just wasn't like other children. He strolled, like a boy in a park without any concern or worry in the world, as if he had on an invisible cloak that could protect him from trouble. Yes, I think it would be reasonable to say... I liked Cameron from the first time I saw him.

*

The bus dropped us right outside the school and we made our way to the main entrance. We had all had a day looking around Titfield last term, so we knew where the year 7 classrooms would be as well as important places like the canteen and the toilets. Everything was much busier than I was used to in a school. There were pupils bustling everywhere, some of them very tall and intimidating. At Prince Albert, we were the biggest boys and girls, but now we were very small new fish in a very large pool full of massive fish.

We walked down the main corridor and saw the friendly face of Mrs Deanus. She had caught sight of us through the hubbub and was beckoning us over with a wave.

"Good morning, boys!" she greeted, "And how are we all this morning?"

I decided to answer on behalf of all of us.

"There was a minor problem at the bus stop, but we're all excited to get started now. Oh, and Stephen is a little upset after an incident this morning where he saw his Mum's vagi…"

"Neil!" bellowed Stephen, digging me in the ribs with his elbow.

Thankfully, the clamour in the corridor was such that she hadn't really heard me anyway, and she ushered us into classroom 7D. The classroom was welcoming with bright displays about the Tudors on one wall, mathematical terminology on another and some French vocabulary and phrases on and around the whiteboard. The back wall had lockers and pegs for our blazers, and all of the desks had been labelled with our first names and the initial of our surname. After depositing our bags, we scanned the stickers to find our places; I was hoping that being Peel and Prince, Stephen and I might be next to each other, but it turned out that he would be behind me. Grub was in the left-hand flank of desks, next to someone who hadn't arrived yet whose name was 'Vijay J'. Grub pointed this out to us, whispering that 'Vajayjay' was the word that his family used for ladies' parts. Stephen groaned at this as he'd had enough of that for a while. It turned out the boy was called Vijay Jayasuriya, and Grub seemed to get on with him well enough; not quite well enough yet to have a laugh about his sticker name though.

I had just taken my seat and was placing my pencil case neatly over my name badge because the top left corner was where I liked it to be, when my eyes wandered over to see who was going to be my desk neighbour. I read the name Ottilie P, and my face began to fall. I'd had to sit next to Ottilie Plank for the last year at primary school, and we didn't get on at all. She was a rich girl, the daughter of Oscar 'Plankety' Plank, the builder who seemed to have built every new house or fitted every new extension in or around Lower Piercing for the past fifteen years. She tended to think that everyone else was beneath her and had a way of putting you down, wobbling her head as she spoke and looking at you as if you were dog dirt on her shoe. Once at the dinner table, Dad had been half-heartedly talking about wanting to do a ten-kilometre race, and I'd interrupted him to say how mean this rich girl Ottilie was. He'd joked that to her, 10k was probably a pocket money proposal rather than a distance, but Ottilie hadn't got the joke when I'd repeated it to her the next day. In fact, her head had wobbled so much as she tutted in disgust that I wondered if it might wobble off.

I was just about to turn to Stephen to let him know of my predicament when Ottilie Plank plonked her bag down on the desk.

"Neil Peel. What the hell?" she snarled. "Of all the sad sacks in this school, I get stuck next to the saddest of them all…again!"

She drew an imaginary line down the centre of the desk with her finger and bent over to look into my eyes.

"This is the line you do not cross. You breathe in the other direction, and you speak to people on the other side and keep your feet under your own chair. Got it?" She then spun around and went to console herself with a friend. "Oh, Remi, you won't believe who I've got to…"

"Nice to see you too. Did you have a good summer, Ottilie?" I whispered as she left, turning towards Stephen.

I opened my mouth to speak to Stephen but hadn't noticed his desk mate sit down during Ottilie's vitriolic tirade against me. I didn't get any words out, although my mouth remained open, and my eyes widened. Next to Stephen was a girl, but this one didn't seem spiteful like Ottilie at all. She wore a serene smile as she looked around the room. She had her wavy blonde hair down loose apart from one section that was pulled into a high ponytail. She looked magnificent, perhaps the most beautiful person I had ever seen. I hadn't met her eye or else I would have looked like a gawking maniac, but I continued my rotation around as far as Stephen who was staring straight at me expressionless. He reminded me of a match stick; his bright, new white shirt made a stark contrast to his red hair and even redder blushing face. Poor thing, I thought to myself. How's he going to get any work done sitting next to that goddess whose name, as I would discover later, was Fleur Poucette.

Just then a bell rang.

"Welcome, everybody. Please find your seats," urged Mrs Deanus, chuckling to herself nervously as she shuffled to the front of the classroom. The chatter died down, and my first term at Titfield School began.

Chapter 4
Visiting My Grandparents

One weekend in early October, we were due a family visit to see my grandparents. My father's parents have a three-bedroomed house, and in the past, Lemony and I had managed to bicker enough while sharing a room to the point that visits had become one-day occasions rather than overnight stays.

During the two-hour car journey to Nanna and Grandpa's (Nanna insisted on having that spelling rather than Nana as she said that 'Nana Peel' would have been too close to 'banana peel' and, therefore, silly), Dad was lost in Rock FM songs on the radio, humming away, tapping on the steering wheel and letting go of the steering wheel to do air guitar solos at key moments. Mum was asleep as usual, having the knack of being able to doze off within minutes of departure and then nodding forwards and jerking her neck back upright at regular intervals. Whenever my hand or knee crossed over the halfway point of the back seat, Lemony would poke me with the tweezers from her make-up bag. Little digs didn't really hurt, but they were enough to incense me into placing my hand right next to the centre and extending my little finger, millimetre by millimetre until I had encroached onto her territory. Wearing a bored expression, Lemony tucked her shoulder-length brown hair behind her ear, then slowly reached across and pinched my finger hard with the tweezers.

"Ouch!" I cried, "Lemony just pinched me with tweezers!"

There was no point in disputing my claim, so she acted hurt and irritated.

"Well if you'd keep to your own side and stop prodding and annoying me, then you won't have to wake Mum up with your whining."

"Stay on your side, there's a good lad," said Dad, looking at us in the rear-view mirror, "and please don't tweeze your brother, Lemony. We're not too far away now."

The DJ called for a 'big shout out to the hard of hearing' before *Deep Purple's* opening riff announced *Smoke on the Water* as the next song. "Oh choon!" exclaimed Dad, clearly judging that his refereeing role was finished.

Despite my general loathing of my sister and her reciprocal feelings for me, we had become strangely complicit in these rare, sole instances when there was an opportunity to play tricks on our extended family. This is not to say that we don't love them; of course we do. My grandparents mean the world to me and have always doted on both of us. They have taught us card games such as 'Whist' and 'Newmarket', where we use Nanna's collection of ancient coins for stakes and to bet on the outcome. There is a special feel to visiting one's grandparents which is difficult to describe to others, but it's something that makes you feel safe and loved.

*

On a similar visit last year, we had found the spare keys to Grandpa's car while rooting through the kitchen drawers to see what treasures we could find. He had been about to go out to the DIY shop, and so Lemony and I had come up with a plan. We'd told Nanna that we were going with Grandpa and so ran out ahead to the car. We'd opened the boot, and I'd climbed in, clutching the spare keys. Lemony had closed me inside and then returned to the house telling Grandpa that we'd changed our minds and would see him later.

Secluded in the boot, I'd felt the engine start and then the car reverse out of the drive. The plan had been to remain in

31

the boot until we stopped at the DIY shop before letting myself out, getting into the back seat and waiting for Grandpa to return, telling him that I'd run the whole way behind the car to remind him that Nanna had wanted him to pick up plenty of sweets for us.

I think Grandpa must have given my dad his love of rock music because he was playing some tunes from the seventies while singing along in a most amusing, tuneless way and commenting on the songs to himself.

"Freddie, you are the duke, nay the God of rock!"

"Oh yes! This intro kicks ass!"

I had never heard my grandpa semi-swear and had to bite my hand to avoid laughing and giving myself away.

A moment later, we'd swerved suddenly to one side, braking sharply and rolling me around in the boot. Grandpa had shouted, "Get off the road, you turkey twizzler! Don't give me the finger you daft whazzock!"

As the next song had finished, Grandpa announced that he too could 'rock the Kasbah' before letting out a fart that grew in intensity over about five seconds. He'd burst out laughing at his infantile joke and comical wind sound, and I'd stifled my own laughter once again. I suppose you never know what a person gets up to in the privacy of his own vehicle, and I felt a little ashamed of myself at intruding on Grandpa.

Everything had gone smoothly, and I'd hopped out of the boot in the DIY shop's car park once I was sure that Grandpa had had long enough to totter out of sight of the car. A lady in a neighbouring space stared at me in disbelief as I clambered out, smiling at her as I changed positions. I had to waft the car's back door a few times, as the fart was pretty intolerably beefy, before locking myself back in.

Grandpa had come back with his fertiliser and lawn seed and almost dropped them on seeing me there.

"Neil! What are you doing here?" he'd exclaimed.

The only part of the plan that wasn't perfect was that I couldn't lie about having run behind the car. I just told him that I'd been behind him the whole time, and he probably interpreted that as meaning in the back seat. He'd blushed a little, apologising for any language that might have been inappropriate and for the 'A1 whizzpopper' he'd let out. We'd both laughed at that, and he'd let me sit in the front on the way back.

*

I looked across at Lemony now, wondering how she could switch so easily from being so hateful to having fun with me. I wondered if I would ever understand my sister or girls in general for that matter.

We finally got off the motorway and headed into the countryside towards the village where Nanna and Grandpa lived. Before long, we were pulling into their drive as Mum woke up with a start and frantically checked her reflection in the mirror, clearing her dry throat and expressing surprise that we were there already.

Nanna and Grandpa looked forward to our visits so much that they had probably had their noses pressed against the window for the past half an hour, and they scurried through the front door, flinging their arms open to embrace us all. Grandpa had a habit of letting out a little laugh as he greeted us, even though nothing funny was happening. It was endearing, but I always wondered why he had this nervous reaction with family. He mussed my hair while Nanna commented how I had grown and what a beautiful young lady Lemony was becoming, although she was one of the few who always called her Melanie; she'd never understood why my parents had gone along with the childish version of the name.

"And you look lovely too, Emma," added Nanna as an afterthought to Mum, giving her an air kiss. Mum and Nanna Peel had always got on well enough, but there was always a potential barb in Nanna's remarks about Mum. I think Nanna had hoped for more for her son; she'd once commented that Mum's outfit looked like she was wearing a dishrag in the days when she and Dad were first going out together.

"You're right, Nanna," I added. "She looks much better than she usually does. She always makes more effort when she's coming to see you."

"Thank you, Neil," said Mum, squeezing my shoulder firmly and ushering me towards the front door.

Once inside the house, Nanna presented us with two bowls of cocktail sausages, regular or honey and mustard. There were enough to feed ten hungry people as Nanna was never one to under-cater. I took two on a cocktail stick out of politeness rather than hunger.

"Careful, Neil, or you'll get even fatter than you already are," sniped Lemony, grinning.

"Aww. He's lovely," replied Nanna, enveloping me into her giant bosom in a solid embrace.

Once we'd gone through the usual questions about how the new term had started and the new friends I'd met etc., there were two options: we could go for a walk or watch one of the old black and white classic films that Grandpa had recorded onto grainy VHS tape twenty years ago. Mum and Dad said that they wanted to stretch their legs and stroll around the village after having been cooped up in the car for hours, and Nanna was keen for her afternoon constitutional. I was about to suggest that I'd go with them too until Lemony put her hand on my arm and said that we'd stay to keep Grandpa company and that *All About Eve* sounded like a super film. She met my eye with a glint in her own, a silent indication that she was up to something…

As the front door slammed shut, we sat down opposite Grandpa who was sitting back in his reclining leather armchair. I'd enjoyed spinning round in this and pulling the footrest out until Mum told me I'd break it if I kept fiddling and, therefore, I was banned from using it.

"Well, Grandpa. I have to make my subject choices for my exams this year," said Lemony, keeping her voice quiet and monotonous. "I find geography quite interesting as there are both the human and the physical aspects. The rocks and boulders and the geology side of it are all so fascinating."

I realised what she was up to; she was hypnotising Grandpa who'd been used to having an afternoon nap for a few years now and so Lemony was boring him to sleep. He looked at her between blinks. His blinks got longer as she continued, and the glances shorter. Then, once the final blink had lasted thirty seconds, Lemony's flat expression turned into a smile, and without breaking her monologue, she continued, "And I didn't even need to mention glaciers. Neil, fetch the sausages and follow me."

We tiptoed out of the lounge and headed up the florally-carpeted staircase, avoiding the fifth step which notoriously gave a creak if you stepped on it. At the top of the landing, she stopped, looking gleefully in front of her. It was Nanna's doll's house.

This was something that Grandpa had built just before Lemony was born. They had lovingly wallpapered all of the little rooms, spent a small fortune furnishing it and even installed electric lighting. The main doll was called Rowena, although there were several other characters there too: a baby in the nursery, a postman, a delivery boy and a maid. I know that Lemony had wanted to play with the house when she was a little girl, but she had always been told that it was for looking at rather than playing with. Nanna or Mum always had to be there to supervise, and whenever she'd picked up a doll, it was swiftly removed from her hands and returned to where it was before she had taken it with a "Yes. That one goes just here."

"What are we doing?" I asked her.

She turned to look at me, brandishing her tweezers and snapping them closed like a crocodile's jaws.

"We're replacing the dolls with sausages, of course," she whispered as if it were the most obvious question in the world.

We set to work stripping Rowena of her outfit and covering a chipolata with the very same clothes. Lemony pinched two eyes and a mouth into where the face should have been using her tweezers and lifted the tiny toilet seat to put the offcuts inside like mini sausage poos. I had to stifle my giggles at that.

"She really is Ro-wiener now!" I blurted as quietly as I could, and Lemony shushed me through her own laughter. Half a sausage was all that was needed for the baby, with more offcut turds in the chamber pot. The delivery boy was easy, and we used two sausages for the maid who was sitting on the sofa. The only problem was the postman on his bike as the sausages wouldn't balance, even when we leant them against the side of the house. I crept back down the stairs and slipped into the kitchen, opening the fridge door. Bingo! There I found a pack of full-sized Cumberland sausages and cut one free with the kitchen scissors. I sliced half of the sausage lengthways down the middle and, hey presto, our new postman would have legs. I was delighted with this discovery and dashed back up the stairs. Unfortunately, I forgot about the fifth stair and put all my weight right in the centre of it creating what sounded to me like a bang as loud as an atomic bomb explosion.

"Is that you, Neil?" asked Grandpa sleepily from the lounge.

"Yes, Grandpa. I'm just...going upstairs to drop off a sausage," I winced, cursing the fact that my honesty might drop us into trouble before we'd had the chance to enjoy our prank fully. I glanced up to the top of the stairs to see Lemony looking thunderously down at me. If I screwed this up, then she would never trust me on such ventures again.

"Okay, well, make sure you flush afterwards, and open the window a bit too," said Grandpa before snorting a little and snuffling back to sleep. Yes! Saved by an accidental euphemism.

Lemony took the sausage from me, and her evil smile slowly returned as she dressed it in the postman's uniform. She slid it onto the saddle, put its hat on and leant it against the wall successfully. Our work here was almost done. We took the naked dolls and hid them at the bottom of Nanna's underwear drawer. The only question was when she would discover them and the sausage fest that was going on in Ro-wiener's house.

We crept back into the lounge and managed to settle down in front of *Bette Davis* well before Mum, Dad and Nanna got back or Grandpa woke up. Lemony had primed me that she should answer if we were asked what we had been doing while they were out walking, but the question never came, and so we played board games and had a hearty roast safe in our delinquency.

As we waved goodbye through the car window, I almost felt bad, but we hadn't done any real harm; the touch paper was lit, and we could wait for Nanna's reaction from a safe distance. Mum snuggled into her seatbelt for her return nap, and I looked across at Lemony with a smile only to see that, for her, the diversion was now in the past; the sneer had returned, and she had resumed her usual disdain, using her tweezers to poke my right hand which had strayed at least three centimetres onto her side of the back seat.

Chapter 5
Incidents with Bullies

October drew on; the mornings got colder and darker, and it was only just light as I left for school. I'd gradually got used to a much bigger school, although I was still discovering new corridors and classrooms.

Ottilie remained a Plank in my side, much more painful than a mere thorn, but at least, she had made a fool of herself by asking if I could get "much more *stupider*" after I'd accidentally brushed her arm with mine while turning to ask Stephen if I could borrow an ink cartridge. Mercifully, we had a few lessons during the week when we went to other rooms, and so I could sit next to different people. One of my favourites was Design as I was partnered up with Grub who was immense at planning and executing his ideas, so I could ride in on his coat-tails; my contribution to our project of combining celebrities to represent contrasting views was to come up with the name Gandhi Warhol, and Grub set to work, creating 'our' masterpiece on the 3D printer. We earned a solid A grade for that.

Vijay Jayasuriya spent some break times with us, but he was far too interested in team sports to be a full-time best friend. Not that he was good at sport, but he wanted to be in with the sporty boys, so if the weather was fine and there was a huge game of football going on, then he'd disappear as soon as the break bell went. Vijay often began sentences with "To be honest", "To tell the truth" or "I'm not gonna lie" which I just didn't understand. Of course, I didn't need to use such phrases, but to me, they suggested that he was usually lying with this time being an exception.

He'd been the unfortunate victim of Basher Walker during a PE lesson which, for some reason best known to the teachers, was not taught in forms but in groups named after colours. We were in the blue group, and it was the only lesson I shared with Walker. We were practising handstands in our gymnastics module, and we were all paired up at various stations around the sports hall, taking it in turns to help each other achieve the desired position, using the wall for balance if needed. Walker had made it as difficult as possible for Vijay to assist him, helicoptering his legs around unnecessarily wildly and then grinning maliciously after he'd knocked his partner into the wall before switching roles. The PE teacher, Mr Lashley, was helping me to hold Cameron's legs still when all of a sudden there was a dull thud and a shout.

"Vijay's flashing his vajayjay!"

There was poor Vijay, face down with his bottom exposed for all to see. He was flipping and flapping around like a landed fish trying to pull up his shorts and pants, while not daring to turn over in case he showed more than just his buttocks. There were shrieks of astonishment and disgust from the girls around the hall while Walker was laughing hysterically and pointing at the hapless Vijay.

Mr Lashley dashed over to the scene in an attempt to help Vijay regain any scrap of dignity that he still had and then dragged Walker and Vijay away towards his office. Walker protested that Jayasuriya had wanted to flash the girls and that it would never have crossed his mind to debag his partner in the middle of a handstand.

*

Cameron had become a good friend which generally kept Walker and Batesy away from us at break times. We were now like the Four Musketeers: Porthos, Aramis, Athos and Zorro.

Batesy may have been in 7D with us, but he was just a powerless sidekick without his bullying friend. We had a very traditional Maths teacher called Mr Campbell who referred to all of us as Master or Miss which was fine for all of us except when it came to Bates. However, Mr Campbell was certainly not going to change his ways because of a bunch of giggling school children, and so Maths lessons became a source of entertainment for all of us except Batesy who tried to keep very quiet in that particular subject. Maths was probably my favourite subject; I'd even got three protractors, so I had all the angles covered.

One morning, before Mrs Deanus had arrived in the form room, Batesy had tried to earn some sort of respect in the class by calling out that Ottilie Plank was ugly. She had cut him right back down to size by calling him a weedy rat-weasel, but I could tell that she was upset. She looked at me and said, "You always tell the truth, Peel. Am I ugly to boys?"

"On the inside or the outside?" I replied.

"My face, you freak," she whispered back in an attempt not to be heard.

"It depends," I continued. "Some days, when you manage to smile, I'd say you were approaching average."

"Oh wow. You're hardly a snack yourself. Take a short walk off a long pier," cursed Ottilie, stomping off to find Remi and not caring to hear that she'd made a mistake with her insult and that I should be taking a long walk off a short pier. Stephen had overheard our conversation and tapped my shoulder in congratulation.

*

Wilberforce was not so fortunate at avoiding bullies as we were. His break time routine was too predictable as he would make his way to the school tuck shop as soon as he got out of lessons to buy as much Battenberg cake as his allowance would permit him. Walker and Batesy saw him as an easy target, especially as he was unlikely to retaliate. He often had bruised shoulders where Walker had dished out punishment, but it seemed to be law of the jungle that you didn't tell tales.

One lunch break, Vijay came rushing over to the banter bench, our spot around the playground, where Stephen, Cameron, Grub and I were chatting.

"Guys! Guys!" he exclaimed, panting. "You've got to come and see this!"

He was gesticulating wildly while explaining that Wilberforce had left his jacket draped over the back of his chair in the lunch hall when he went to get seconds of pudding. Walker, who was sitting at the next table, had filled the pockets with custard and Wilberforce hadn't noticed until he got up to leave, putting the jacket back on and plunging his hands into the cold custard.

"And Wilberforce has flipped!" continued Vijay. "He's challenged Walker to a fight in the spinney!"

There was clearly no time to lose, so we hurried down towards the sports hall where the wooded copse surrounding it, usually known as the spinney, was about to become a boxing arena. There was already a decent crowd gathered, and I could see two figures in the middle. Wilberforce had adopted an old-fashioned boxing stance and was circling Walker whose usual snarl was mixed with a hint of amusement. I was about to burst into the man-made boxing ring and try to break up the would-be pugilists when Stephen put his arm in front of me.

"Just hold on a second," he said, looking at Wilberforce's determined features. "Don't stop him. This could be the day when Basher gets a taste of his own medicine, where Goliath finally…"

"Oooh! Me cartilage!" spluttered Wilberforce, crumpling to his knees as Walker bopped him right on the nose.

"Okay. Maybe today is not that day," muttered Stephen as I pushed past his arm.

"Stay out of it, Neil," called Grub, "or he'll whack you as well! He's not called Basher for nothing, you know."

But I'd had enough of the injustice, and seeing an innocent knocked down spurred something inside me. I strode towards Wilberforce and helped him to his feet; he had a trickle of blood flowing from his left nostril.

"Oh, look," began Walker. "Fat Gollum's here to take his bum chum to the hospital so they can both get liposuction."

"Four syllables. I'm impressed, Walker," I answered. "But let he who is without a big nose make the first suggestion for cosmetic surgery."

There was an audible intake of breath from the assembled crowd and a few sniggers too. I knew I was on dangerous ground here, but anger was winning the battle against rational thought.

"You're really asking for it, Peel," warned Walker, taking a step towards me. "What makes you so full of yourself?"

"Well, I can't be full of anyone else, can I?" I replied.

There was another collective gasp and a few more titters, but I could see that my time was running out. Batesy stepped up to Walker's shoulder, trying to look as tough as possible. Walker bunched his fists as if getting ready for round two with a different opponent.

"Funny boy, eh? Always got a punch line. Try one more, and it'll be the line where I punch you."

Just then, the attack came from an unlikely source. Batesy must have had a sudden rush of blood to the head as he stepped forward and swung a punch at my stomach. I'd never been in a proper fight and so did not really know how to react. Impulse made me curl up my arms like a praying mantis, and Batesy's blow struck me on the elbow. My bone seemed to be much more solid than his fist because he was the one who clutched his right hand, yelping in pain as the school bell rang, while a slight tingling in my funny bone was all that I felt.

The crowd dispersed, and we scarpered towards our maths lesson, leaving Walker cursing Batesy for being 'an interfering tool'.

"Well done, Neil," exclaimed Grub. "You nailed Batesy. I'm sure he was just about to cry."

"I'm hardly the next Muhammad Ali," I replied. "I was lucky. The next time, I'll end up flat on my back with a broken nose."

Even Wilberforce made it to the maths lesson looking unscathed. He had cleaned up his bloody nose and gave me a small smile of gratitude. Batesy, however, appeared to be in pain and could not grip his pencil properly to do his calculations.

"Oh. Come, come, Master Bates. Whatever is the matter?" enquired Mr Campbell. "I've had enough of seeing your knuckles shuffling clumsily across the page. That's rather a loose grip."

Scowling towards me, Batesy replied that he'd fallen and hurt his hand at break time, so Mr Campbell sent him to the school nurse to get some ice on his 'swollen digits'. I was preoccupied during the rest of the lesson, worried about having got into my first fight and what kind of a reputation I might be getting. Would others assume that I needed taking down a peg or two and want to fight me?

I'd gone through far fewer questions than everybody else by the time the bell rang, so Mr Campbell said that I had to finish all of the work at home and submit it first thing in the morning. This was fine as I was good at maths, and the topic was not really difficult at all.

Dad asked about my homework later that evening, and so I told him all about the incidents of the day. He listened and told me he was proud that I had done the right thing in standing up to injustice, although he also looked concerned about the attention that had fallen on to me, advising me to be careful and to stay away from Walker in future.

I decided that it was time to head upstairs, so I glanced around the kitchen door and blew a kiss to Mum who was busy talking on the phone. She gave me a distracted wave, her brow furrowed in concentration on her conversation. As I trudged up towards the bathroom, I heard her say, "Okay, I'll ask him." She then called up to me. "Neil!"

"Yes, Mum," I answered, turning back to the top of the stairs.

"It's Nanna Peel on the phone," she continued, smiling up at me. "She's asking if you might know why the dolls in her doll's house have been replaced by pork products. Apparently, the postman has started to turn green and has mould-hair."

"Oh yes," I said, remembering our little stunt with a grin. "Lemony and I thought it would be funny to put sausages in the dolls' clothes. The dolls are in Nanna's underwear drawer under her pants, the big pairs, that is, not the one that was way too small for a bottom like hers."

But Mum had already gone back into the kitchen to apologise to Nanna. I saw that Lemony's door was ajar and so decided to tell her that our misdemeanour had been discovered, but just as I was about to knock, the door was pushed closed from the inside. I took the hint and went to bed.

Chapter 6
Half Term

The half term eventually arrived, and I certainly needed to recharge my batteries. The transition to Titfield had been smoother than I'd anticipated, yet the school days were slightly longer. In fact, I was so tired that I was still fast asleep when Mum shouted up to wake me at half-past ten on the first Saturday morning of the week off.

"Neil! Auntie Sue's here."

Blinking my way into the day, I remembered Mum saying the week before that her sister was coming to stay for the weekend. I didn't mind Auntie Sue, but Lemony couldn't abide her; she was devoutly religious and had never married or had children of her own, and so she had an awkward way with young people. Each birthday, she'd send a card, but instead of money or a present, she'd put in a slip of paper with a bible verse written on it. Lemony said that this was a waste of time, as that was a voucher that couldn't be exchanged in any clothes shop. We don't go to church as a family, and Dad certainly is a firm atheist, but at least Auntie Sue is always positive, and you couldn't spend more than two minutes with her before she'd give one of her hearty, nasal, snorty laughs.

"Here's my favourite nephew!" cried Auntie Sue, putting down her handbag and overnight case and throwing her arms wide open in anticipation of a hug before noticing that I was in my pyjamas.

"Oh. Wakey wakey, rise and shine. The sun's burning your eyeballs out," she offered, laughing to herself. She wrinkled her eyes behind her round glasses at her own lightheartedness while enveloping me in a semi-reciprocated cuddle, her short, greying hair tickling my nose. "You've got so big! Come and sit down, and tell me all about how your new school is going. Where's your sister? Is she still in bed as well?"

"I'm not sure, Auntie Sue," I yawned. "I was so tired that I really only woke up when you rang the doorbell."

"Well, Emma," continued Auntie Sue, turning to my mum. "Is Lemony still in the Land of Nod?"

"No," replied Mum. "She went out early to her friend Ella's house."

"But didn't you tell her that I was coming?"

"Well, yes, I did," stumbled Mum, realising that that was why Lemony had got up so much earlier than she ever did on a Saturday morning. "But she'll be back soon."

I was encouraged to eat breakfast and dress quickly so that we could go for a walk around Lower Piercing before lunch. We set off at a brisk pace, and Auntie Sue immediately took my hand in her vice-like grip, singing 'This is the day that the Lord has made' to herself. Even though I was eleven years old, it did not cross her mind that holding hands might have been potentially embarrassing if we'd come across any of my friends or, even worse, my enemies. I'd foreseen this eventuality and had worn my woolly hat pulled down low so that my face was barely visible. Even if we had passed anyone from school, there was a good chance I would not have been recognised. I got a very good view of the fallen leaves swirling around in the autumn breeze. I even spotted a dog poo and steered Auntie Sue deftly around it. She smiled at me.

"Thanks for the dirt alert, Neil. Guide me o thou Great Redeemer!"

Miraculously, however, the village was very peaceful, and we managed to avoid crossing paths with anybody I knew. I breathed a sigh of relief as we arrived back home, and Mum unlocked the door for her sister.

No sooner had we walked through the door than Auntie Sue screamed and stumbled backwards, almost knocking me over as I was trying to take my shoes off. She made the sign of the cross on herself before pulling out her own crucifix necklace and pointing it into the entrance hall.

"Stay behind me!" she shrieked. "A demon walks abroad in this house!"

"What the devil are you talking about, Sue?" cried Mum who had also been pushed into the coat rack.

"Devil indeed!" she continued. "Behold!"

Auntie Sue stepped forwards so that Mum and I could see what had created such a fuss. There, at the bottom of the stairs, was a banshee in dark, dirty rags. Demonic yellow eyes protruded from pale grey skin and tangled bushy hair, not to mention the fangs that protruded from her canine teeth!

Just at that moment, Dad came out of the kitchen.

"Back from your walk?" he said. "What do you think of Lemony's Hallowe'en outfit? Isn't it great? The yellow contact lenses are perfect."

"There is no Lemony. Only Zuul," growled demon Lemony in as low a voice as she could muster.

"Oh Lord, Lemony," exclaimed Mum. "You scared the daylights out of us."

"John," said Auntie Sue, trying to regain her composure. "Are you really allowing her to dress in that unholy costume?"

"Oh, it's only a bit of fun, and she spent hours getting ready," replied Dad.

"Well, I have very sore misgivings," announced Auntie Sue, crossing her arms in front of her chest and not daring to glance away from Lemony.

"Would you like to borrow some Vaseline for that, Auntie Sue?" I asked, trying to be helpful. I wasn't sure what 'misgivings' were, but I used Vaseline when I had sore lips, and there were so many code words among girls and women that I assumed this was another one.

Lemony finally broke out of her character and sniggered before turning around and heading upstairs to change. Auntie Sue needed a cup of tea and a good sit down to recover, and she still didn't seem quite ready to trust Lemony when she eventually came downstairs out of costume. I resisted any comment about how she was far more frightful like this, although I would have had to admit that her outfit was pretty terrifying.

We sat around the dining room table for lunch, and Lemony had a wicked gleam in her eye. She had scored a great first point over Auntie Sue and seemed keen to press her advantage. She met my eye as she took a burger from the middle of the table and began to add condiments. I had a feeling that I knew what was coming as I remembered the last time that Lemony had tormented Auntie Sue, who could not abide even mild swearing, by telling her about Ella's new dog, which was a Shih Tzu. She had mentioned the breed name many more times than was necessary before seemingly changing the subject and telling the joke about what do you call a zoo with no animals? Auntie Sue hadn't even waited for the punch line before standing up and storming away, saying, "I pray for you, Lemony. Really I do."

"So, Neil has been telling you about how school has been going, has he, Auntie Sue?" said Lemony, calmly.

"Yes. It sounds like he's got some good friends. How about you...?" started Auntie Sue before Lemony interrupted her.

"I was wondering if they'd test him to see if he had Asperger's."

"No," I stated. "These are beef burgers, not ass burgers. Who would eat ass burgers?"

Dad snorted with laughter and almost spat out his mouthful of burger as Mum lowered her head into her hands. Auntie Sue's smile melted away as she put her fingers in her ears, closed her eyes and stood up singing *"Stand up, stand up for Jesus!"* to drown out the sound.

"Lemony! Neil!" said Mum firmly. "Go and eat in the other room."

Dad was desperately trying to remain responsible, avoid sniggering and keep his food in his mouth as we picked up our plates and left the room, with a mixture of shame and pride.

*

The following day was Sunday, so Mum went to church with Auntie Sue, although we were not obliged to go as Mum thought we might do or say something to upset her sister again. I'd arranged to have lunch with Stephen, and then we were going to head down to the river to meet up with Grub and Cameron afterwards. It was good to see everyone in a setting away from school. This was *our* tree by *our* stretch of river, and we dumped our bikes and relaxed, lying back in the dry, still leaves, our coats done up tightly against the cold. I told the boys about my Auntie Sue's visit, how Lemony had scared her half to death and the dinner table incident.

Stephen and Grub hadn't been up to much yet, but Cameron had been to see the latest Spiderman film and said how it was better than the previous versions.

"I don't watch those films," said Grub, thoughtfully.

"Why not?" asked Cameron. "Don't you like action films?"

"I think I've got arachnohomophobia," Grub reflected.

"Is that a fear of Spiderman?" I asked.

"Or a fear of gay spiders?" added Stephen.

We all laughed at that, revelling in the stress-free camaraderie. Cameron had got up and was lobbing stones and twigs into the water.

"Pull me up, Cameron," asked Stephen, holding his arms outstretched. Cameron obliged, but Stephen only allowed Cameron to lift him about six inches off the ground before letting out a ripper of a fart. Cameron dropped him immediately and stepped backwards, holding his nose in his gloved hand.

"Oh my God, that stinks!" protested Grub.

"Pure Chanel number 2," said Stephen, gleefully wafting his fumes towards us.

"That's toxic!" I added. "*You* must have been eating ass burgers."

"What can I say?" offered Stephen. "I'm a badass."

"You *have* a bad ass, Stephen," said Cameron. "Plus, that sounded very wet. Do you need a pitch inspection to check there was no liquid?"

"All safe," concluded Stephen, patting his bottom.

Grub grabbed the tree rope and swung out twice in perfect semi-circles, hoisting himself at the key moment both times to avoid the nutcracking notch.

"I'm creating a draught to get rid of that gas," called Grub.

"Fight fire with fire and wind with wind, eh? I like it," approved Stephen.

Just then an all too familiar and unpleasant voice signalled the arrival of Walker.

"Well, well, well, Batesy. Looks like we've found the Butt-Munch society headquarters. Council is in session with Fat Gollum as president and Bread Stick swinging around to provide ventilation."

Batesy and Walker had cycled up behind us and dropped their bikes. Walker was flicking his penknife blade out and back again. We all looked at each other, annoyed that our safe haven had been discovered by these two bullies. Stephen stood up, with Grub shuffling quickly behind him, abandoning the rope swing.

"Leave us alone, Walker," he said defiantly. "We've got no beef with you."

"Beef...beef?" considered Walker, standing close to Stephen. "Well, perhaps I've got a bit of beef with you."

Stephen's breath billowed out visibly in the cold air. I stood up too, moving to his side.

"Look. It's bad enough to have to smell your breath. I don't want to have to see it too," insulted Walker. "I dub thee Corpse Breath. Yes, that's it. We've got Fat Gollum, Bread Stick, Corpse Breath and perhaps I'll dub you Crotch Cheese," he added, glaring at Cameron.

I really wanted to avoid conflict, so I tried to think of a way of diffusing this unpleasant situation.

"You should be careful about dubbing everybody. Nicknames stick," I suggested light-heartedly. "One of my Dad's friends misread the word 'cockles' when he was younger, and he's been known as 'Cockless' ever since."

Walker turned to face me, smiling. "That's a good one. I like that," he said softly. "Perhaps, though, you might want to shut your mouth if you know what's good for you. You do know what's good for you, don't you, Fat Gollum?"

"The last I heard, it was five portions of fruit and vegetables per day, but advice changes," I answered, honestly.

"Hmmm," muttered Walker, taking a step towards me and flicking his penknife again. "You always have to get the last word in, don't you, Fat Gollum?"

"We're all human beings here. Maybe it would be better for everyone if you re-*traced* your steps, and we can all go our separate ways," proposed Cameron calmly, holding Walker's gaze. I thought he was being cryptic again, but this wasn't the moment to ask him about his jedi-like influence over the bully.

Walker reflected on this, stepping back from me. Batesy looked from Walker to us, waiting for his orders. Between the two of their heads, in the distance, I could see a figure cycling along the riverside path towards us. I jolted in the realisation that it was my auntie Sue! Mum, Dad or Lemony must have told her where we hung out, and she had decided to take an afternoon bike ride out to see me. I tried to think of an outcome that wasn't horrendous but was struggling to find one. I started shifting my weight from foot to foot with nerves as Auntie Sue got steadily closer.

Walker seemed to have finished his deliberations and announced that he wasn't going to hurt us. He simply wanted the old rope that was hanging from the branch of our tree and took out his penknife blade to show how he meant to detach it.

Auntie Sue was probably about five hundred metres away and gaining now, so I had to act quickly.

"Here's my offer," I said, the others turning to look at me, confused. "I bet you can't swing around in a perfect semi-circle like Grub just did. If you can do that, including a perfect dismount, then you're welcome to take the rope."

"I'll tell you what," threatened Walker, as Batesy grabbed the rope from my hands. "I'll do a perfect swing twice, dismount any way I choose, and then cut the rope down anyway."

A look of menace had returned to his eyes as he closed the knife and put it loosely in his pocket, grabbing the rope from Batesy. Auntie Sue was about three hundred metres away now and had spotted me, apparently having fun with my five friends. She waved, and I could just make out a joyous smile on her face.

Walker stood at one end of the rope's arc, grinning as he prepared himself. He threw himself forwards, and, as soon as he'd set off, I watched Stephen, Grub and Cameron all look upwards towards the branch. Walker may well have been physically strong, but he did not know the physics of this particular swing, and so he had launched himself at the wrong angle. He was just over halfway through his arc when the rope rode up onto the notch and then dropped him with a sudden jolt. I saw a look of pain and panic in his eyes as he shouted out a swear word.

"Coo-ee! Neil!" called Auntie Sue, not hearing Walker's expletive.

He had lost all concentration and also the grip on the rope. Walker was desperate to dismount, flailing his legs as he completed his swing. Batesy tried to grab his floundering friend, but Walker was off-balance as he landed and ended up pulling Batesy into the icy water on top of him with a mighty splash! I grabbed the rope and swung it as hard as I could so that it coiled around the branch tightly, safely out of reach.

"Ow! My knackers!" cried Walker, grasping his crotch. "My poor balls. Holy sh...!"

"Christ, it's freezing!" shouted Batesy.

Auntie Sue was just about to arrive when she heard Walker's foulmouthed tirade and lost her balance as she was trying to block her ears and come to a stop at the same time. She teetered over her bike as it collapsed on the path, and she too lurched down the bank and fell headlong into the river with a mighty splash!

"Jumping jellyfish, that's cold!" she exclaimed.

"That's my auntie Sue," I whispered to Stephen as we scrambled up to collect our bikes and pedal away home. I stopped where she had gone into the river and helped to pull her onto dry land, checking back to see if Walker and Batesy were coming after us. They, however, were both still searching in the water, and I could hear Walker berating Batesy for not having seen where his penknife had fallen and landed.

Auntie Sue suggested going to help my two friends who had also fallen into the river, but I explained that they were not my friends at all and that they would only swear at us if we tried to help. She agreed that she had heard more than enough bad language for one Sunday, and so we cycled back home so that she could change clothes and warm up in front of an open fire.

Chapter 7
Lesson in Love

I was in love with Fleur Poucette.

This girl had been sitting behind me and next to Stephen for half a term now, and I had barely shared more than a handful of sentences with her. Frankly, I didn't really dare to speak to her in case I made a fool of myself. I knew she had a French father, and I'd found myself researching what her name meant. Fleur was the French word for flower, and apparently, Poucette was something like the French version of Thumbelina, which was appropriate because she was quite petite.

We had discussed various things in groups of four in lessons, but that usually meant Ottilie trying to take over and look down on Stephen and me. She tried to be pally with Fleur, but Fleur never showed any favour to Ottilie over us, and that made me love her even more.

She had a normal English accent, but her father spoke to her in French so she was bilingual. Of course, she was top in French class and was used as a demonstrator by Mademoiselle Bosworth, our teacher, in any oral work so that we could attempt to imitate her perfect accent. Our French lessons would often include pair work, and this was usually difficult, since Ottilie wouldn't speak to me. She would look at her textbook or the board and pronounce the dialogue to herself, not letting me join in the conversation. If we were chosen to read aloud, she would read her line and then turn to look at me as if I were stupid.

I wasn't naturally good at French, but I wanted to do well in every piece of work or test, just in case Fleur ever

54

heard the results. Perhaps that was silly, but it played on my mind anyway.

On the first day back after half term, Stephen had gone for a dentist appointment, and Ottilie had not come back from her skiing holiday yet, so I had a place next to me and so did Fleur. Our French lesson was about places in a town, and we had been practising some keywords before moving on to a dialogue. Miss Bosworth had displayed the dialogue on the board and asked us to read it through in pairs.

"*Fleur, mets-toi à côté de Neil, s'il te plaît,*" said Miss Bosworth.

"*Oui, Mademoiselle,*" Fleur replied, before bringing her books and pencil case and sitting down in Ottilie's place, smiling at me as she did so.

"*Bonjour, Monsieur!*" she pronounced in her perfect accent.

"Err…*Bonjour, Fleur,*" I replied, staring at her and beginning to blush.

"No," she giggled. "That is the first line of the dialogue. You are supposed to say '*Bonjour, Mademoiselle*'."

"Oh yes. Sorry," I smiled back and tried my best with the rest of the passage until we got to the word '*rue*' for 'street'. I must have mispronounced it slightly because Fleur picked me up on it.

"There are two different sounds for words that have a 'u' or 'ou' in French. This one is as if you are trying to say the sound 'ee' through kissing lips," explained Fleur. "Look at me and make a kissing shape with your lips."

My heart rate immediately leapt as I puckered up. Fleur was doing the same just a foot away from my face, pinching in her mouth with her fingers. Her pale blue eyes were so captivating that I was completely lost within them.

"Now try to say 'ee'," she continued, demonstrating the word '*rue*' with a perfect rolled 'r'.

I must have made a decent attempt through the haze that had overtaken my brain because she said, "Well done, Neil," putting her hand on my forearm as she did so. Fleur was far more relaxed about gestures such as that than the rest of the class. I would never have dared to touch a girl's hand or arm like that, but it was nothing at all to Fleur.

Mademoiselle Bosworth was working her way around the class, listening to the various pairs, and she eventually arrived at us. We gave our rendition of the work, and I tried very hard on the word '*rue*', looking to a smiling Fleur for approval.

"Bravo, Neil," encouraged Miss Bosworth. "You are like an onion in French lessons lately."

"Oh. I'm sorry, miss," I answered. "My mum said I should start using deodorant."

Miss Bosworth and Fleur both laughed, although I wasn't aware that I'd made a joke.

"No!" replied Miss Bosworth. "I didn't mean that at all! I mean you are using layers that we talked about to learn the language. Add some new words weekly, learn them with our 'Memrise' system, do well in your tests, and now you are working on the pronunciation too. Layers like an onion. This is all really encouraging."

"Thank you, miss," I said.

"Mademoiselle," added Fleur. "*J'aime bien travailler avec lui. Il est trop mignon.*"

I wasn't sure quite what she'd just said, but I think it was something nice. The rest of the lesson continued in the same way. It was the most torturous yet wonderful thirty-five minutes of my life thus far; I couldn't wait for it to end, yet I couldn't bear for it to be over. I said nothing about it to Grub and Cameron over lunch until Vijay Jayasuriya came past on his way to play football.

"Wow! I had to take my jacket off in the French lesson, Neil. You made the temperature go up by at least ten degrees working with Fleur. At one point, I thought you were going to kiss each other. Nice one, mate. Hot stuff!"

With that, he ran off to join the footballers, just as Stephen came over to our bench.

"Did I miss anything this morning, guys?"

Cameron and Grub looked at me and then back to Stephen again.

"Not really, mate. How are the teeth? Have you got ginger-vitis?" asked Grub, smiling knowingly at me.

Stephen explained his dental appointment, but I had drifted off into thinking about the reason for having a girlfriend at my age. Should I ask her out? Where would we go? What would we do? What if she said no? What if Stephen liked her and wouldn't speak to me again? What would everybody else say if they knew? How could I avoid saying that I was madly in love with her if anyone asked?

At the age of eleven, I'd decided that there were too many potential pitfalls in this game of love, and so it was for the best if nothing further was said about it. I could truthfully answer any questions by saying that Fleur was very nice and far more mature than anyone who might be thinking of teasing me. I would not be able to relax properly around her, but my love would have to wait a while until I knew just what to do about it.

Thankfully, Grub and Cameron did not press the subject any further either, and so Stephen did not find out about my stolen romantic French experience with his desk mate.

It was the first secret I had had from him.

*

At the end of afternoon break, I was heading to my locker to gather my things for the next lesson when Stephen grabbed me by the shoulder and spun me around.

"Neil. You have to come and see this," he said with a note of urgency in his voice.

I left my locker and followed him out of the classroom and down the corridor. Eventually, he stopped and faced the notice board in front of us.

"Look," he commanded.

I stared at the board, trying to see what was so important. There seemed to be team sheets for various matches as there were every week, but I didn't see what Stephen was getting at until he pointed at one particular notice. There usually fixtures for the Under 12 A, B, C and D teams, but it seemed that this week, there was a match for the Under 12 E team. That couldn't be right; there were only enough boys in the year group to make an E team if…no…it couldn't be. I scanned the list of names: Pearson, Prince, Dufresne, Grubman, Jayasuriya, Pudge, Bates, Peel. Nooooooooo! I looked at Stephen in despair.

"Don't worry about it, Neil," he soothed. "Mr Lashley knows that you're not keen. That must be why he's got you down as number 8 on the list. You probably won't have to play."

I wanted to believe Stephen, but I thought it would be far safer to get my name off the list altogether, so the school nurse would have to come to my rescue. It was too late to see her now, as the lesson was about to start, but I wasn't going home without stopping in first before I left for the day. My concentration was poor at best during the remaining lessons of the day, and as soon as the final bell rang, I gathered my things together at top speed and told Grub and Stephen that I'd catch up with them at the bus stop.

It was a relief to see that nobody was waiting to see Mrs Beever in the medical centre, and her door was wide open. I knocked politely to draw her attention away from the computer screen.

"Hello, darling. What can I do for you?" she inquired in a caring, matronly way.

"Well, Mrs Beever," I began. "I was hoping you might be able to tell Mr Lashley that I can't play in the Under 12 E team tomorrow."

"Oh, you poor lamb," she replied, "Why's that? Are you feeling poorly? I can give you a spoonful of milk of magnesia. Have you tried for a poo?"

"No. It's just that I *really* don't want to play," I explained as convincingly as I could. "You see, I really don't like football and would make a complete fool of myself if I went out there. Surely that's against my human rights or something."

"But you aren't ill or injured in any way?" asked Mrs Beever.

I was beginning to think I should have gone about this in a different way, telling Mum or Dad that I didn't fancy it and asking them to write me a note. They could have lied for me, and as long as it hadn't been me saying the words, I think I could have reconciled that with my conscience. However, it was too late for that. My reckless spontaneity had got the better of me.

"No," I replied quietly, lowering my head.

"Then you'd better get ready to play tomorrow. Titfield are counting on you, young man. Just give it your best shot."

Dammit!

Chapter 8
The Football Match

If I had to be involved in the match, then at least I was happy to see my name as number 8 on the team sheet. Even my limited knowledge of the game extended as far as the fact that the eighth man in a seven-a-side game was a substitute. My plan was to stay among the supporting parents and out of sight of Mr Lashley so that he didn't ask me to go onto the pitch. That was probably his plan too, and since he would be busy refereeing the game, everything ought to work out fine. I'd told him that neither of my parents would be attending, so he should feel under no pressure to 'give me a run out'.

Autumn leaves peppered the dewy turf as we strode out in single file onto the pitch in our yellow shirts, blue shorts and long yellow socks. Stephen had tucked his shirt in and pulled his shorts right up for a joke giving him what Lemony called a 'camel-toe'. Cameron's Mum had bought him new boots for the occasion, and they were clearly biting into his feet as he couldn't walk more than four paces without bending down to pull at them. Grub looked around nervously, pushing his glasses up his nose.

Mr Lashley gave us a ball to pass around in a small circle, but we all stopped when the opposing team from Badby, bedecked in a purple kit, got off the minibus and made their way over towards us. We all seemed to freeze in terror at the sight of one of their players. He was as tall as Mr Lashley and he had the manly adornment of a downy shadow above his top lip.

"Jeez!" quivered Stephen, "Look at the size of him."

"He's a big unit all right," replied Cameron, "he'll be the one to smash your specs, Grub."

"Oh great," said Grub, "Now I can relax into the game, knowing that they've got Gigantor playing centre forward."

Eventually, Mr Lashley waddled over to us and gathered us around him in a huddle. The disappointment and shame were evident in his voice as he tried to encourage us.

"Now, listen, lads. You're the Under 12 E team of Titfield School, and that's something to be proud of, isn't it, so go out there and give 'em all you've got."

As he turned to shake hands with the Badby coach, I heard him mutter that it would be a bloody miracle if we did anything other than lose 10-0.

"Be careful out there," I said, "I don't think Gigantor could actually kill any of you, but he looks like he wants to hurt someone quite seriously."

Mr Lashley tooted his whistle, and the game began. Cameron took the centre and immediately lost possession to Badby.

"Come on, Titfield!" shouted a lady next to me. Pearson, our goalkeeper, recognised his mother's voice and turned to wave at her. Gigantor, meanwhile, was making his way forward with the ball. Grub leapt deftly out of his way. Stephen pretended to offer a leg for a tackle but withdrew it just in time. Mr Lashley, panting to keep up with the Badby brute, noticed that Pearson was distracted and shouted.

"Pearson! Face the ball!"

Pearson turned back to the game just as Gigantor released a thunderbolt of a shot that slapped him full in the face.

"I didn't mean literally face the ball," said Mr Lashley as Pearson crumpled under the blow.

"Oh, my goodness. He's just had a brace fitted," exclaimed Mrs Pearson as Grub helped the dazed goalkeeper to his feet.

"Great save, Pearson," I shouted encouragingly.

The onslaught continued with Badby laying siege to the Titfield goal. As half time approached, the score incredibly remained 0-0 with Pearson and the posts coming to the rescue time after time. Then Gigantor picked up the ball in midfield again and galloped his way goalwards. Pearson had taken a fair old battering, but he wasn't giving up. He crouched and steadied himself to prepare for the shot, but his reactions were not fast enough to stop the ball homing in on his groin.

"He got him in the area," I remarked.

"This time it was in his penis," said Mrs Pearson's neighbour.

"Man down!" shouted Stephen.

"They've mashed his spuds!" offered Grub.

Mr Lashley blew the whistle for half time, and I ran on to join the crowd of my teammates that had gathered around Pearson, who was quite pale and also in tears.

"Tough luck, Pearson," I said. "A whack to the testicles can ache for two hours or even longer in extreme cases. That must be why he's upset, sir."

"Thank you for that, Peel," exclaimed Mr Lashley. "Of course, that means that *you*'ll have to replace Pearson in goal."

"But, sir! I just don't want to," I protested.

"We've no choice. Pearson can't play on, and you're the substitute so don the gloves. You're in goal for the second half."

I gulped and looked around for some means of escape but realised that I was trapped, and I would have to take my place on the pitch with my band of brothers.

Thankfully, pounding Pearson and our posts seemed to have tired Gigantor somewhat, so he was more subdued for the first ten minutes of the second half, and indeed I didn't have to touch the ball at all. In fact, Vijay even managed to move the ball into the Badby half on three separate occasions. I offered advice to my defenders, mainly suggesting that they tackle Badby, but then, eventually, Gigantor seemed to have found a second wind when he received the ball from one of his defenders. He started to get up a head of steam, as I took a step to the left of my goal. As he brushed passed Wilberforce, I took another pace to my left, edging away from the danger zone. Grub offered little resistance, clutching his glasses as Gigantor flew by him; again, I inched to the left. I could see spittle arcing from the brute's mouth, his face red with frustration at not yet having scored. He was about to wind up his shot, and I was standing more or less in line with my left post, offering him the whole empty goal.

From the side of the pitch, I heard a voice that was perhaps more highly pitched than usual.

"Don't let him score, Peel, you doughnut!" yelled Pearson.

He had perhaps sacrificed his chances of becoming a father to take one for the team, and, for a split second, that must have stirred something inside me. Against my better judgement, I started towards Gigantor with an animalistic roar building in my throat. Was this to be my moment of heroism? I noticed a split second's worth of hesitation on Gigantor's face just as I stood on my own bootlace, which I had neglected to tie properly. I couldn't lift my left leg and spun as I fell pathetically to the ground.

Fortunately, my trajectory ended right in front of the goal, so the striker's shot struck me clean on the left buttock, and the ball bounced away to temporary safety.

"Ow! That will almost certainly leave a red mark!" I shouted at Gigantor, pulling myself back to my feet.

The Badby goalkeeper was camped out on the halfway line, bored of having had nothing to do for so long. He moved up to the loose ball and was aiming a hefty boot at it. Poor Grub, who had been waiting away from the danger zone, was right in the way and didn't have time to manoeuvre his way to safety. Instead, he put his hands over his glasses and raised one leg, contorting himself to protect his vitals.

The Badby goalkeeper did catch the ball very sweetly, but it struck Grub right on his bony kneecap and ballooned up in the air towards the Badby goal. Twisting in horror, the Badby keeper slipped and fell to the turf as Grub opened his eyes and realised that he had an open goal in front of him. Now, he may have been small and skinny, but Grub could run, and so he set off after the bouncing ball. The home crowd began to stir as their belief grew that perhaps the impossible was possible. Grub was now running at his top speed with two Badby defenders chasing after him. The ball was still bouncing in the right direction, and even I, rubbing my tender buttock, felt something close to excitement. Finally, Grub caught up to the ball in the Badby area and swung his boot at it hopefully. However, he had hopelessly misjudged the bounce and missed the ball entirely, pivoting around his standing foot and falling to the ground as he did so. It didn't matter though, as the ball still had enough pace to bobble over the goal line in front of the desperate, outstretched legs of the two defenders.

We had scored a goal.

A cheer erupted from the parents on the sideline, and even Mr Lashley couldn't help but throw his hands in the air and run over to pick up a confused Grub.

We managed to hold on for the remaining three minutes, helped by the fact that Gigantor was blaming the goalkeeper, who was blaming his defenders, who were bickering about who should have been marking Grub. Mr Lashley blew the whistle for full time, and it was all over. I raised my arms to the heavens in delight. It seems that some others were happy that we had won the match, but to me, that was immaterial; the only game of the term was over, and I was still alive.

Chapter 9
Christmas Shopping

The period before Christmas held a special magic for me. Lessons began to get less serious, and the importance of school was replaced by the excitement of the sights, sounds, smells and tastes of all things festive.

From the beginning of December, or occasionally the end of November if he could get away with it, Dad would put little twinkling lights around the house, preferring those to the main lights; he lit candles every day too to add to the special, soft lighting. Sprigs of holly with plump red berries would be hung from the curtain poles and rested on the mantelpiece. Decorations that my parents had kept for years would make their annual excursion from the garage, and there would always be a Christmas jigsaw to which anyone could contribute on the puzzle board. Nat King Cole, Dean Martin, Bing Crosby, Doris Day, Andy Williams and co. would play softly downstairs to add atmosphere; even Lemony didn't complain about having these 'old' crooners on a loop at this time of year. There was usually a bowl of mixed nuts, pretzels or crisps out for snacking and always plenty of satsumas in the fruit bowl and mince pies in the cupboard. Most weekend mornings, Mum would make her home-made buttery, cinnamon puff pastry swirls, which were the taste of Christmas in my mind.

This particular Saturday morning, the house smelled of warm, sweet vanilla and cinnamon due to the sweet vanilla and cinnamon candle that was burning in the kitchen. I had saved up thirty pounds, and today was my Christmas shopping day. I had to buy presents for Mum, Dad, Lemony and a joint present for Nanna and Grandpa, who were due to join us on Christmas Day. Buying for Lemony used to be a pain because she would ask me what I'd got for her as soon as I'd got back from shopping in an attempt to upset me by spoiling the surprise. More recently, however, she had stopped bothering, silently suggesting that whatever I got her would be lame anyway and that she was completely indifferent. She'd enjoyed telling me that she was getting me some stain remover this year so that I could wash in it and make myself disappear.

Stephen and Grub were due to come round any minute, and we were going to take the bus into Lowcester, as there was a big shopping centre there. Cameron was visiting his grandparents and so wasn't able to come with us. Usually, I hated shopping, but I was happy to make an exception once a year. I knelt by the lounge window, scanning the driveway while listening to Nat King Cole singing *Don we now our gay apparel, fa la la, la la la, la la la* and smiling about how I used to wonder who *Don* was and if those lyrics were anything to do with that American television programme about drag queens that Lemony liked to watch.

Just then, I saw my two friends approaching and dashed to grab my coat, hat, scarf, and boots. It was dry outside at the moment, but it was overcast and close to freezing, so I wasn't taking any chances. I checked that my spiderman wallet was in my inside pocket and opened the door hastily. This was not a time and place that I anticipated a deadly attack, but right in front of my face, a hammer was descending towards me, and a man was making a grab for me and wailing! Thankfully, Dad managed to stop himself falling on top of me, and he just pulled the hammer away at the last second.

"Aaagh. That was a close one!" he said, pulling me back to my feet. "I was just putting a tack in the door to hang Franklin on. You scared me, Neil."

Franklin was the name of our wreath; Dad had thought it was funny to name it after the singer Aretha Franklin, and it seemed that I had just interrupted her bedecking of the door.

Having survived a hammer attack, the journey into Lowcester went without incident, and the three of us got off the bus, ready to tackle this task. However, this was the first time we had been allowed to come into town on our own, and, not being keen shoppers, we weren't really sure where to go.

*

In fact, I'd got away with not having to go to the shops much at all since the time when a sales assistant had been trying eye make-up on Mum and had asked me my opinion.

"She looks like my friend Grub did when he had conjunctivitis," I'd replied. "Either that or she's got a black eye."

Mum had rolled her darkened eyes, apologised and ushered me out without buying anything, and that was the last time I'd been forced out when Mum needed to go into Lowcester.

*

I spotted a hardware shop just outside the shopping centre and thought I might be able to get some gardening gloves for Dad there. I found some that looked about the right size and they only cost five pounds, so that was a bargain. After paying, I found Grub looking in the 'Grow your own' section.

"You two know that refers to plants and not body parts, don't you?" came Stephen's voice from behind us.

We chased him out of the shop but then laughed with him as we entered the shopping centre. Glorious displays of coloured baubles hung across the ceiling and each shop had made the effort to make their window look better than its neighbour. Charity collectors shook the change in their boxes and offered stickers with a friendly 'Merry Christmas' to those who donated to the various causes. A life-sized nativity scene was just up ahead with a security guard present to stop people stealing the baby Jesus or riding on the plastic donkey.

A young woman approached us with some flyers for a restaurant.

"Can I give you a flyer? Ten pounds off for parties of four or more."

"It's not worth it," I answered. "I'll only put it in that bin over there straight away. You might as well keep it."

She looked taken aback, but Grub apologised on my behalf and took a flyer from her.

"Why did you take it, Grub?" I asked. "You aren't going to eat there."

"True," he replied, looking at the deal on his flyer, "but she's only doing her job getting rid of them, so I'm helping her out." He paused, reading as we were walking before asking, "Why do they have specials for virgins? I've always thought that was weird."

"What *are* you talking about, Grub?" asked Stephen.

"It says so here on this menu," insisted Grub. "Four meals just for virgins, and they always have them in other restaurants too. I've seen parents ordering them before, so they can't be that strict about it."

"I don't understand," I admitted, baffled.

"Look. Here," protested Grub, pointing at his flyer. Suddenly the penny dropped.

"Grub," I began quietly, starting to smile. "Do you know the difference between a virgin and a vegan?"

"What's a vegan?" replied a confused Grub.

"Oh, yes!" cried Stephen as he realised Grub's error. "That is priceless."

"Look, everybody. It's the vegan Mary," he said, pointing at the nativity scene.

"Okay. Keep your voice down," whispered an embarrassed Grub.

Stephen calmed down but went on ahead of us with a spring of amusement in his stride. After a few more seconds, Grub asked me, "Seriously though, Neil. What is a vegan?"

*

As the clouds got thicker and darker, we continued our shopping, Stephen finding all of his presents at the chemist's, because he bought shower and bath gel for everybody on his list, proclaiming that he'd done all of his Christmas shopping in approximately three minutes, queuing included. Grub was far more indecisive, debating the benefits of headscarves over necklaces for his mother. Stephen offered words of wisdom, telling him not to forget that today's unwanted Christmas present is tomorrow's eBay hot pick. Grub ended up buying her some bath gel, and Stephen was very happy about that. In answer to the Lemony dilemma, I found a T-shirt with the slogan '*I have no idea why I'm out of bed*' emblazoned on the front and thought that she might possibly wear that. She'd probably get me chocolate covered sprouts again, but I was loath to waste my money on a gift that she couldn't use. I bought a mini rocking horse for Rowena's nursery for Nanna and Grandpa before admitting defeat on Mum's present and returning to the chemist's and settling for some bath gel, as recommended by Stephen. Everything bought with four pounds to spare. A victory.

I bounded up to my bedroom to wrap my presents as soon as I got back from Lowcester and hid them in my secret place, at the bottom of my wardrobe, underneath my jumpers. The job was well done, and I was excited to see my family's reactions when they opened their presents. I leant contentedly with my elbows on my window sill, looking out into the twilight over the garden and noticed that snow had started to fall. Those heavy clouds obviously couldn't take it anymore and had decided to empty themselves. The garden was already covered with a light dusting, and the flakes were now falling thick and fast. It must have started while I was wrapping my presents. I opened the window and watched the wintry scene with a smile on my face, enjoying the sensation when one of the snowflakes landed on my face. This was going to be a wonderful Christmas.

The end of term was greeted with elation by everybody in 7D, and Mrs Deanus looked quite emotional as she wished us a Merry Christmas and gave us a small wrapped present that turned out to contain a budget supermarket's own brand malted chocolate reindeer. On the bus journey home, the boys and I discussed the fact that the last few days before Christmas were going to be family time, but that we would surely meet up as soon as possible afterwards, especially if the snow was still around.

I'd barely had a chance to take off my shoes, coat and blazer after I'd got home and said hello to Mum when the arc of headlights swung across the wall, announcing that a car was pulling in to the drive. A moment later, the front door opened again and a branch was thrust through, followed by the rest of a Christmas tree and my dad puffing beside it, his arms clasped around the middle.

"Here we go!" he cried. "A six-footer. A bargain at half the price, but unfortunately it was full price."

"Don't start without me," I said, giving Dad a cheery hug before sprinting upstairs to get out of my school uniform and into my pyjamas and dressing gown. Even though it was only about five o'clock in the afternoon, it had become a tradition for me to help dress the tree in my nightwear, and this was yet another custom that filled me with a warm glow.

By the time I got back downstairs, Dad had got the tree set up in its stand in the corner of the lounge and had cut the retaining strings so that the Peel family Christmas tree could be appreciated in all its lush fullness. Lemony had sauntered in while I was upstairs, since she never walked back from the bus stop with me. It would have killed her credibility to be seen with a year seven pupil, and so she would dawdle behind chatting with Ella and taking her time, even in chilly December. She seemed completely disinterested in dressing the tree and rolled her eyes when Mum said that it would be nice to do something together as a family. There was a plate of mince pies on a side table with four mugs of hot chocolate and a fire roaring in the hearth.

"I'll get the lights in from the cupboard under the stairs, and you two fetch the tree decorations from the shelves in the garage," suggested Dad.

Mum was busy attaching the day's Christmas cards onto a hanging ribbon as I hurried out towards the garage with Lemony following...slowly. I switched on the light and looked up at the shelves. There were three boxes marked 'Tinsel', 'Baubles' and 'Assorted decs', and so I opened the step ladder to reach them. I stood on the top step, stretching to grasp the box marked 'baubles', straining to hook my fingers around it and inching it towards me. I realised I was slightly off balance and a little dizzy but just managed to steady myself when suddenly my whole world went dark.

"Turn the light back on, Lemony!" I shouted, looking at her silhouette framed in the doorway.

"Oh, sorry," she said, sarcasm dripping from her mouth as she flicked the light back on. "I leant on it accidentally."

I scowled at her while stepping down but, in not paying full attention, I scuffed my heel on the bottom step and tripped forwards, breaking my fall by putting my weight on the box of baubles. A quiet crunching noise came from within the box, and I winced at the thought of having probably broken something precious in sentimental value if not in price.

"Careful, clumsy," chided Lemony, smiling at me. "Let *me* get the other boxes in case you break something else."

"It wasn't my fault," I protested. "I wouldn't have dropped it if you hadn't turned the light off."

"Well, I could agree with you, but then we'd both be wrong," she retorted, pushing past me to get to the ladder.

I glumly carried my box through to the lounge before admitting to Mum and Dad what had happened.

"Don't worry," consoled Dad as Mum opened the box to check its contents. "I'm sure it's not too serious."

But it was.

There were only three broken baubles, but one of them had belonged to my mum's parents and had been passed down to her. They had died before I was born, so I'd never known Nanna and Grandad Davies, but there were certain things of theirs that Mum really treasured, not so much expensive heirlooms but sentimental memory items such as the bauble whose pieces she held in her fingertips now. She wasn't saying anything and was just looking down at the debris, but I recognised the robin's head and silvery background. My chest felt tight, and I looked to my dad in despair. He looked back at me with an understanding expression before moving over to Mum and putting his arm around her shoulders. I could see that she was wiping a tear away from her cheek.

"There you are, Neil!" exclaimed Lemony, struggling with two boxes of decorations. "I thought you were coming back to help instead of…"

She broke off on seeing Mum crouched over the baubles, put her boxes down and hurried over.

"Are you okay, Mum? Oh no! Did Neil break Nanna and Grandad's bauble?"

We were all quiet now, the three of them huddled together and me standing apart and alone. I was very upset, but nobody seemed to notice apart from Lemony who shot me a poisonous glance.

"I'm sorry, Mum," I whispered, before turning to leave the room and heading upstairs to my bedroom, feeling like a naughty little boy but also frustrated that Lemony had somehow, without really doing very much, managed to change my excellent mood into a terrible one. I attempted to keep the tears away as I lay down on my bed, trying to imagine what it must be like for my mum. She had no living parents, and her stupid son had gone and ruined Christmas for her. I had been lying there for a mere two minutes before there was a gentle knock at the door.

"Neil, can I come in, sweetheart?" asked Mum.

"Err. Yes," I replied, hoisting myself onto my elbows and then into a sitting position.

Mum came in, slightly red around the eyes but smiling.

"I'm so sorry," she said as she came over to me, arms stretched out to take my hands.

"You're sorry?" I questioned. "I was the one who broke the bauble."

"Yes, but it's only a bauble," continued Mum, looking into my eyes. "Just a bauble. I was sad for a moment because it reminded me of happy Christmases when I was little, but I realised that I don't need an ornament to remember that, and what's important to me now is to make happy times for you to remember. You love Christmas, and what I really want is for you to come back down and help decorate the tree with me."

I held my mum's gaze for a while before giving her a long hug and taking her hand to lead her back downstairs. Dad had just finished wrapping the lights around the tree, and so we were free to start draping tinsel, hanging the intact baubles and finding a sturdy branch on which to perch Robin, the imaginatively-named, fluffy robin. Lemony had got bored and was slumped on the sofa, remote control in hand, skipping through television channels.

The phone rang, and Lemony sprang up to answer it, probably thinking it was Ella calling for her. However, it clearly wasn't as she came back, holding the phone limply and letting it slide into Dad's hands.

"It's your brother for you," she said flatly, barely looking at him before returning to the sofa.

Dad took up the phone and wandered out of the room as he spoke.

"Air hellair! How the devil are you, Peej old squire?"

He had a most peculiar way of speaking to his brother, adopting an upper-class twit's voice which the pair of them seemed to find hilarious. I didn't quite get it. My uncle was called Peter, but that was always Peej on the phone. He had been single for years but surprised everybody three years ago by coming back from a business trip to Romania married! His wife, who was almost half Uncle Peter's age, was called Lexa, although Dad referred to her as Sexa now that her surname was Peel, and it hadn't taken them long to announce that she was pregnant. My first, and so far only, cousin had just had his second birthday, but I hadn't put myself in Uncle Peter's good books after the birth by saying that his pride and joy, baby Nicolae, looked more like a wrinkly walnut than an angel. I revised my opinion later, thinking that he looked more like the Emperor from Return of the Jedi, but I thought it best to keep my thoughts to myself. Now that Nicolae was two and able to talk, Uncle Peter and Auntie Lexa had become those loud and proud parents who made a big deal out of every time the boy peed in the potty or pronounced a new word. I'm not sure that any of his achievements thus far qualified him for child prodigy status, but what do I know?

I was just adding those last few unnecessary extra decorations when Dad came back in, having finished his phone conversation.

"Peej and the gang can make it for Christmas," he said with enthusiasm.

"Yay," replied Lemony from over on the sofa with no enthusiasm at all.

Mum seemed fine about this as long as they weren't staying the night. We already had Nanna and Grandpa staying over, and I was supposed to be giving up my room for them; I'd be sleeping on an inflatable bed in Mum and Dad's room because there was a pull-out bed under my mattress to make my bed into a double. However, after a bit of discussion, it was decided that Uncle Peter would come and stay over in my room and Nanna and Grandpa could come over on Christmas morning as that was the best way to stop Grandpa drinking too much and spending the whole day asleep. The cherubic little scrote, Nicolae, would sleep in a travel cot in my room too. Later that night, just before going to bed, I relocated all of my most treasured possessions to the back of my lockable desk drawer or the depths of my wardrobe, covered in clothes. If I was asked to fetch something for him to play with, it would be the big plastic building blocks from the garage, so my Playmobil pirates should remain safe.

Chapter 10
A Family Christmas

Early on Christmas Eve, Dad and I went to do the food shop. There was quite a bit of snow on the road, and some of it had turned icy. Dad whacked the car's fan on to full blast and looked behind him.

"Reversing," he quipped. "In this weather, that's the way forward."

As he reversed the car out of the driveway, the wheels locked up, and we almost hit our neighbour, Mr Bush's car, coming to a stop mere centimetre away from it.

"That was a close one," I said. "Look at the skid mark we've left."

"Too right that was close," replied a relieved Dad. "I'm not sure that's not the only skid mark that I've left."

I was in charge of the list, and we had gone early enough to get a parking space but not so early that the queues for the checkouts weren't already backing up into the aisles. We were behind an overweight couple who also had a full trolley. The man was the kind who speaks very loudly and looks around to make eye contact, drawing unwitting bystanders into his conversation. His round, shaved head poked out of a dirty Christmas jumper bearing the slogan 'You can pull my cracker', and he also wore a pair of jogging bottoms that sagged to reveal half of his bum. I don't imagine this fellow had ever been for a jog, and the waistband was struggling against the laws of physics to maintain his dignity. I thought of him as Uranus because he was as big as a planet, and you wouldn't need a telescope to see his anus if the elastic of his trousers inched down any further.

"Halloumi?" he announced to his wife. "You wouldn't catch me eating that foreign muck. What's wrong with good, old-fashioned British cheddar or brie?"

My dad moved a packet of smoked salmon over the two packs of halloumi that were in our trolley but made the fatal mistake of making eye contact with Uranus. He repeated to Dad, "I sez to our Maureen. I sez: You wouldn't catch me eating that foreign muck. What's wrong with good, old-fashioned British cheddar or brie? What you need is some good old red meat and 'taters'. That's how you get big muscles, isn't it, feller?"

He then seized my biceps and gave me a squeeze.

"Actually," I replied, pulling my arm out of his grip and picking out one of the packs of halloumi from our trolley, "Brie is foreign. It's from France, and we buy halloumi all the time."

Perhaps Dad could sense that I was about to tell Uranus that he could do with cutting back on the 'taters', so he delved into his pocket and pulled out the car key, thrust it into my hand and sent me back to wait in the car while he apologised on my behalf.

*

"Lord St John Smythe!" exclaimed Uncle Peter as he stepped in through the front door that evening.

"What what, Peej, old boy!" answered my infantile, 43-year-old father, embracing his brother. There were 'Merry Christmases', kisses and handshakes all around before Dad helped Uncle Peter to bring in the cases. Lemony was keeping the peace with her presence, putting up with false affection because it was Christmas. Perhaps there would be some malice to keep her entertained in good time. Soon the kitchen that Mum had tidied to within an inch of its life was covered with plastic bags and toys. The star of the show,

Nicolae, was sleepy and so hid his face in Auntie Lexa's shoulder.

"Ah! Has Nicolae gone shy?" cooed Mum. "Where's a cuddle for your auntie Emma?"

"Auntie Em, Auntie Em!" mocked Lemony, turning to head back upstairs. "Where's Toto, Auntie Em?"

Auntie Lexa stared after Lemony before looking back to Mum and smiling.

"He's not really shy, just a bit timid. He'll be ready for cuddles when he's woken up properly. Look, Nicolae. There's your cousin, Neil. Come and say hello, Neil."

Reluctantly, I shuffled over. I'd known that it would be expected that I would entertain him so that the adults could have their time together. Lemony would, no doubt, be shut up in her room for most of the evening and would be able to wriggle out of having to spend any time with Nicolae if that was what she decreed.

Auntie Lexa grabbed me around the waist and squeezed me into her ample bosom, close to Nicolae.

"Careful you don't smother the poor lad, Sexa," quipped Dad.

As Mum was chiding Dad for his remark, Nicolae let go of the handful of his mum's V-neck jumper and gripped my ear hard, snaking one of his skinny, little fingers right down my ear canal. I struggled to pull away, but he just clutched me even tighter and dug in his fingernails.

"Ow!" I shrieked. "He's got me by the ear."

All of a sudden, Nicolae turned his head around and burst into laughter, making everyone else smile and laugh too. Everyone except me that was. I was in agony and in fear of permanent deafness, but his grip was strong for a toddler, and the ear is a very delicate body part. Since nobody was going to help me, I took hold of little Nicolae's wrist and pressed hard with my thumb in an attempt to loosen his grip. Finally, the pain abated and he let go of my ear, but his laughter had turned into a howl and a flood of tears.

"Way to go, Neil," said Uncle Peter, tending to his son.

"But the little sod nearly burst my eardrum!" I cried. I was incensed about being turned into the bad guy for merely defending myself.

Auntie Lexa turned away from me and muttered something in Romanian that didn't sound very complimentary.

"Okay. That'll do," soothed Mum. "How about some nibbles and a drink, everybody? And Neil. Could you fetch something for Nicolae to play with perhaps?"

"He must have something of his own in one of these bags. There are so many of them," I pointed out, rubbing my sore ear.

However, nobody had a chance to say anything else before a voice from behind me announced:

"Here you go, Nicolae. Look what Lemony found at the bottom of Neil's wardrobe. Some little people for you to play with."

"Oh, yes. Fank you, Lemony," gurgled Uncle Peter in a babyish voice, crouching to Nicolae's level and waving his arm for him. Nicolae stopped crying and chuckled, grasping towards Lemony.

"Aw!" echoed the other adults whilst I stood stunned in the middle.

"No!" I cried. "They're my special pirates, and it said ages 4+ on the box. He's too young!"

"Oh. Don't be silly, Neil," said Lemony. "You never play with them anymore, and besides, look at his little face."

She was holding up pirate Sid and Inky Bubbles, the octopus, but I knew that they had been arranged carefully at the bottom of the box so that everything could fit in just how I liked it. She'd obviously taken the time to seek out my favourite figures with which to entice him. Uncle Peter took Nicolae from Auntie Lexa, stood him on the floor and led him by the hand towards Lemony who held out Sid and Inky Bubbles. Nicolae took the octopus and Uncle Peter took Sid.

"Aaagh, me hearties!" exclaimed Uncle Peter in his best pirate voice and wiggling Sid from side to side. "It's Captain Blackbeard."

"No, it's not. It's pirate Sid," I objected, but nobody heard me over Nicolae's laughter as he took Inky Bubbles and repeatedly bashed Sid over the head. His cutlass fell to the ground, but nobody seemed to notice as Uncle Peter and Nicolae hurried through to the lounge where Lemony had dumped the rest of my precious toys.

I picked up the lost cutlass and looked at Dad, imploring him to do something but he just shrugged his shoulders impotently and said, "Come on, Neil. It's Christmas." He then went back to getting everyone a drink. Inside I was furious, but I realised I wasn't going to win this battle. Perhaps I didn't play with them anymore, but this was my favourite childhood playset, and it was the principle that counted. I'd just have to go and watch over my demon cousin and hope that my toys were sturdy enough to last the evening.

In the lounge, the whole pirate set was spread out across the rug by the fire, and Uncle Peter was in the process of putting the wrong hats on the wrong pirates and giving everyone the wrong weapons. Nicolae had pushed the pirates' Fishgutter ship over and had already emptied all of the little gold pieces out of the treasure chests. It was chaos, but he'd gone back to examining Inky Bubbles quietly, so I decided to give everyone back the correct hats and weapons under the guise of playing with them. Whilst in the middle of finding the correct sword for pirate Barnacles, I began to notice a strange smell.

"Stinky poo poo," giggled Nicolae, but this didn't smell like poo. I glanced over at him. He was perched on the edge of the sofa, holding Inky Bubbles and looking at me while biting his bottom lip with a naughty expression on his face.

"What is that? It smells toxic," asked Uncle Peter.

Nicolae pointed to the fireplace and said, "Stinky bubbles in da fire."

I looked where he was pointing and could see a bubbling, black molten blob of rubber with a narrow tube coming from it. This was sitting on top of one of the flaming logs, and horror struck me as I realised that the little devil had detached Inky Bubbles' rubber squirter from inside his plastic shell, and it was now burning away to nothing.

"Inky Bubbles!" I screeched. "What have you done?"

"That was not a good boy thing to do, Nicolae," said Uncle Peter calmly as Nicolae grinned back at him without shame. "We'll have to get Neil a new one now."

"You can't," I shouted in desperation. "They don't make this version of the pirate set anymore, and the new one doesn't have an octopus in it."

As I was talking, I was gathering my toys together and dropping them into the plastic box. I was furious, and Uncle Peter could tell. He even prised Inky Bubbles away from Nicolae and put him back in the plastic box. I knew that something like this would happen, and my frustration was bubbling up to a boiling point. I balanced the Fishgutter on top of the box and carried it to the doorway. Nicolae was still looking at me, and he still had an amused look on his face.

"You're a stinky poo poo," he said to me quietly, clapping his hands.

I'm not proud of it but my anger had reached a crescendo, and I used a bad swear word.

"Shut up, you little twat!"

As I stormed up the stairs, I heard Nicolae repeat the word 'twat', and Uncle Peter called after me.

"Thanks for teaching him that, Neil."

I carried my toy box and pirate ship into Mum and Dad's room where I would be sleeping and hid them under the bed for safekeeping. Just as I was returning to close the door and shut myself in, Lemony appeared.

"That was aggressive," she said calmly. "You're supposed to be nice to everyone at Christmas. Goodwill to all men and all that."

"Says who?!" I exclaimed angrily, flushing scarlet with irritation.

"Jesus, I suppose," she reflected before turning around and walking back to her bedroom singing *Joy to the World*.

I was already in my pyjamas by the time Dad came up to see me.

"Oh, Neil old boy," he said. "That was a shame, wasn't it?"

"If you're going to have a go at me for swearing, then I'm not in the mood," I replied.

"No," he said, holding his hands up in surrender. "I meant a shame about the squirter. He's only two years old. He didn't mean it."

"He did it on purpose," I continued. "Why doesn't anyone tell him off properly? If there was any justice, he wouldn't get any presents tomorrow, but I bet he'll get a sack full."

"Now, cheer up, Neil," Dad replied, trying to sound as soothing as possible. "It's Christmas Day tomorrow, and Nanna and Grandpa are coming over. We'll have a nice family day, and you love Christmas, so just put this behind you and look forward to your presents."

Dad pulled me into a hug, and I did, momentarily, feel a bit better. I brushed my teeth and settled into my inflatable bed and tried to get to sleep. My mind, however, had other plans, and I spent the next couple of hours turning the day's events over and over. Was I spoilt? Did I deserve to live with Uranus and 'our Maureen' in a world where there was no halloumi? Would I really have noticed if Inky Bubbles' squirter had been missing for the past three years? What were Nicolae's redeeming features, and could I find some way to like my cousin? I was finally drifting off to sleep when a shout from the bathroom pulled me back to consciousness.

"Stinky poo poo! I done a poo."

"Shh, Nicolae! You'll wake Neil up, and he'll be grumpy again," whispered Uncle Peter.

Grumpy again? Too right I'd be grumpy. My seething rose but then gradually ebbed away again, and I was just floating off to sleep when Mum and Dad came in, followed about five seconds later by the smell of booze.

"I can't see anything, Emma," whispered Dad, loudly.

"Keep your voice down, love," replied Mum, in a slightly softer whisper. "You'll wake Neil."

I could feel Mum stepping past me towards her side of the bed before she let out a hiccup.

"Oh no. I've got the hiccups now," she sighed.

"Do you want me to give you a fright to cure you?" asked Dad.

"Oh God, John," retorted Mum. "Will you put some pants on?"

I groaned internally, glad that I was facing away from their bed.

"But I always sleep nekkie," protested Dad.

"Not tonight, Josephine," replied Mum.

There were then some shuffling noises amongst Mum's hiccups before a sound like a muffled, angry duck quacking startled me.

"John. That's vile," scolded Mum.

"Merry Christmas," chuckled Dad. He then must have lifted his feet to waft the air out of the bottom of the duvet because I was hit by the full force of his beery fart. Mum was right. It was vile. I held my nose until I thought the worst had passed, but I was wrong and had to hold it again while blowing the foul air away at the same time. Within a minute, Dad had fallen asleep and was snoring deeply. Mum had somehow fallen asleep, even though she was still hiccupping, and now both of them were farting every couple of minutes. It was like wind tennis, Dad's deep rumblers versus Mum's little squeakers. I took sanctuary by putting my head under my own duvet to escape the disgusting symphony that was taking place in my parents' bed. How on Earth was I supposed to fall asleep?

The last time that I checked the clock, it was showing 03:14, so I must have drifted off eventually.

*

"Wake up, sleepyhead. It's Christmas!"

Daylight was peeking around the curtains in the room as I blinked my way out of my slumber, and slowly I realised that I must have slept late if the sun was up on Christmas morning. Mum was standing over me with the welcome prospect of a bacon sandwich in her hand.

"You were sleeping so soundly that we didn't want to wake you," she said, "but Nanna and Grandpa will be here soon, so you'd better get up and get ready."

"Have you done presents yet?" I asked eagerly.

"Well that's the other thing, and you have to promise not to get angry," said Mum cautiously. "Your cousin woke up very early, so Peter took him downstairs and let him open his presents. Pete said Nicolae was happily playing with his new toys, so he closed his eyes on the sofa for a moment, and when he opened them again, Nicolae had opened all of your presents too."

"What?" I cried, suddenly wide awake.

"It's okay, love," smiled Mum. "We managed to salvage most of the wrapping paper, and we've taped them back up again. He did rip the pages out of a Dungeons and Dragons book that you got, so I'll get you another one of those, and he snapped the spear from a little lead goblin figure. Try not to be too upset."

"Why does he have to be such a pest?" I asked. "And can they please not come around again? I don't like him."

"He's only little," answered Mum. "Now, come on. Eat your bacon sandwich, and come and open your presents."

I tried to calm down while eating my traditional Christmas breakfast and then hurried downstairs, excitement rising within me. I wasn't going to let a little toad ruin my Christmas.

"Here he is! Merry Christmas lazy bones," called Uncle Peter who was already slouched in front of the television with a can of lager in his hand. He tossed me a soft, rewrapped present across the room, which I dropped. Everybody was already up, although Mum and Dad were fussing around in the kitchen, preparing lunch with Auntie Lexa. Nicolae was playing with his toys at his dad's side.

"Thank you," I replied, opening the present to see a blue football shirt inside it. "Oh. Well, that's not perfect since I hate football and will probably never wear it."

"You're welcome," answered Uncle Peter, taking a swig of his beer, his eyes never leaving the television. He wasn't listening to me. "Those shirts are only three quid in Romania. A bargain."

Nicolae came over to me and took my hand, pulling me towards where he had been playing. I noticed that he had little coloured square stickers on his T-shirt and face.

"Look, Neil," he said earnestly, reaching up to stick an orange sticker on my nose. "Faver Cwissmas, Faver Cwissmas."

I looked to see where he was getting the stickers from and realised that it was a Rubik's cube.

"Isn't Nicolae a bit young for one of those?" I asked.

"Oh, yes," replied Uncle Peter, glancing down. "I'm afraid that's one of yours, but he didn't want to let go of it, so we didn't rewrap that one. You don't mind, do you?"

What more could this little monster do to annoy me? My uncle's attitude stank too. I didn't want to ruin Christmas, but I had to answer the question honestly. Before I had a chance to roar my answer, I noticed that Lemony had sauntered into the lounge behind me.

"Why don't you tell Nicolae about *Faver Cwissmas,* Neil?" she suggested quietly.

Of course. Thanks, Lemony!

"Faver Cwissmas isn't real, Nicolae. There is no Faver Cwissmas! If there was, you wouldn't have got any presents."

Uncle Peter spluttered out a swig of beer as he reached to cover Nicolae's ears. Nicolae, however, was already in tears. I wasn't sure if he had understood me properly or if he was just crying because I appeared angry, but Lemony had given me a method to vent my frustration. After all, honesty is the best policy!

*

85

My outburst had soothed my anger a great deal, although when I'd looked around to see if Lemony was enjoying the aftermath, all I saw was her back as she slowly walked out of the room; her work here was done. Almost everything she did was calm and slow, yet deliberate. I was torn between wondering what she was like in a PE lesson and pondering what she could achieve if she used her genius for good instead of evil.

A word of reassurance and a quick cuddle with Uncle Peter had soothed Nicolae, and they had soon returned to playing with toys and watching television respectively. I opened my other presents, and apart from a spearless goblin, a pageless book and a stickerless Rubik's cube, I also got a device to change your voice into a Darth Vader-style voice, the usual Matchmaker chocolates and selection box, some films, some vouchers, some books with pages intact, some clothes and a sew-your-own tapestry with the message Jesus loves you from Auntie Sue. Our local Christian Aid charity shop would be glad of that last one.

Mum and Dad both seemed happy with the gifts that I'd got them, and Lemony seemed to smile a little when she opened the T-shirt that I'd bought her. She even managed a 'Thanks, Neil' since Mum and Dad were standing right next to her. She got me a box of Ferrero Rocher, but I could tell it wasn't genuine since the 'chocolates' were not wrapped very professionally. It was no surprise to find that she had eaten all of the actual chocolates and used the foil wrapper to cover sprouts. She gave the broadest smile I'd seen from her in weeks when she looked at my 'not surprised' reaction upon opening the first Rocher, and I suppose this twist on predictability was quite amusing.

Nanna and Grandpa arrived just before lunch to more hugs and 'Merry Christmases' as they stamped the snow off their shoes. Thankfully, Nicolae went shy at new arrivals, so it wasn't all about him for a brief moment. Nanna had knitted a yellow jumper for Lemony, and she announced that she'd had enough of the same wool left over as I was opening my present to discover that I, too, had a lemon-yellow jumper. She insisted that I try it on, but she had clearly not had quite enough spare wool as it only covered as far as my belly button.

"Oh well. Thanks for trying, Nanna," I said.

"It'll be all right if you just pull your trousers up a bit higher," suggested Grandpa. "Like this."

He lifted his jumper up to show a shirt that was straining at the buttons over his bulging stomach and a pair of dark trousers that rose up far higher than was normal.

"I don't know much about fashion, but that's hardly the look that young people are going for these days, Grandpa," I replied.

Mum brought in more presents, and Grandpa looked pleased with his new handkerchiefs.

"Thanks, love," said Grandpa. "I've had the same hankies for years, and 'snot funny anymore."

He winked at me for approval about his puerile joke. I smiled and gave them the rocking horse for their doll's house.

"Fetch my specs from the kitchen unit, would you, Neil?" asked Grandpa. "I can't see the detail on this horse without them."

"You're getting old, Dad," said Dad. "You'll be 75 next year, won't you?"

"Grandpa doesn't look 75," I interjected. "He looks about the same age as Mrs Brady from down the road, and she's only 72."

"No, she's not," replied Lemony. "She's 86."

"Oh," I said quietly and went to fetch Grandpa's glasses.

*

I set the table just as the meal was almost ready. Grandpa came in from the lounge at the last moment and offered to help. He had a habit of doing this just as there were clearly no jobs left to do.

"Would you like me to make my famous onion sauce?" he asked.

"Not today, love," answered Nanna. "It doesn't really go with Christmas lunch."

"Oh," he said turning to me and smiling. "I can do amazing things with onions, Neil. I can make your hair curl with my red onion chutney and my raw onion salad would make your eyes water."

He chuckled at his own joke, and I laughed along too. I had probably heard it several times before, but I liked the familiarity of his humour. Grandpa went over to where Nanna was stirring the gravy.

"Have you put any redcurrant jelly in there?" he asked.

"I do know how to make good gravy," replied Nanna, indignantly. "Now buzz off and stop being a pest. I've been making gravy for as long as I can remember."

"As long as you can remember? Surely, it hasn't been that long," I said, toying with the image of Nanna doing nothing else except making gravy non-stop since the age of four.

"At our age, you can't remember longer than five minutes," replied Grandpa. "In fact, who are you?" he jested. I noticed a glint in his eye, or it could just have been a cataract.

"I'm fine, thanks, who are you?" I said, stealing his punchline before hurrying away from his inevitable tickling.

"Neil, can you fetch everyone in for lunch?" called Mum.

*

Lunch went by without incident, and then intentions to play a board game afterwards disappeared quickly as most of the adults fell asleep on the sofa while Nanna entertained Nicolae in the snow in the garden. Lemony was in her room listening to the new *Durty Dreamz* CD that she had got for Christmas, and I watched the *James Bond* film, which I could just about hear over Grandpa's snoring.

Uncle Peter's family had to go home late in the afternoon as they had people coming to stay with them first thing in the morning. I couldn't bring myself to thank them for the useless football shirt they'd given me, but I did manage to say, "I suppose I'll see you again soon."

I hoped it wouldn't be next Christmas if they remembered my Father Christmas outburst.

Once they had gone, I moved my presents and belongings back into my room and was annoyed, if not really surprised, to see that Nicolae had used his felt-tipped pens to design a constellation of coloured marks on my wardrobe door; his travel cot had been positioned just there, and this was his parting shot to me.

This had not been the ideal Christmas by any means, but I'd overcome the stumbling blocks and was still smiling. Very soon I'd be back with my friends again.

Chapter 11
Haircut

Mum had decided to make a commitment to yoga her New Year's resolution, and she had a group of friends who began to come around late in the morning on Saturdays. They had been meeting occasionally in the months before Christmas, but no one was taking it particularly seriously, so this new dedication was supposed to help them feel better and help lose a few pounds after the festive indulgence. They each brought a mat and would stretch themselves out while listening to relaxing music. The lounge was out of bounds during these sessions as Mum got embarrassed after I said that she looked like a dog peeing up a lamp post in one of the poses. Dad thought it was hilarious to put his hands together as if in prayer and bow while greeting the visiting ladies and say 'Namaste', pronouncing it to rhyme with 'paste' rather than 'a stay'.

I hadn't had a haircut since the beginning of September, and so I was well overdue a trim before starting the new term. Unfortunately, we'd left booking anything rather late, so my usual Turkish barbers had no availability on the final weekend of the holidays. I'd have to go to Mr Steinberg's, the ancient Lower Piercing traditional barber who knew only one cut: the (very) short back and sides. He offered walk-in appointments, and so Mum sent me off with the requisite ten pounds. She couldn't come with me to limit the damage as the yoga ladies were due around and that *rendez-vous* could not be broken. I'd tried to protest, but my hair was well over my ears and collar, and I could pull it down to touch the tip of my nose at the front.

Begrudgingly, I zipped up my coat and plodded off towards the village centre, a sense of dread mounting with every step. I had to mince gingerly along as the snow had compacted into ice for much of the journey. Steinberg had a reputation for having no mercy on his customers/prey and boys older than I was had been known to leave his premises in tears, even leaping off the seat halfway through the cut and sprinting out of the door to safety. Urban legend said that his father, Steinberg senior, had cut hair for the Nazis during the Second World War, and that rumour had even twisted as far as to claim that he was Hitler's personal barber. I didn't believe a word of that as Steinberg junior was clearly Jewish but he was certainly feared by the young, despite his age.

I turned the corner into the main street and could see the dreaded, old-fashioned barber's pole with the red stripe rotating around the white pole like a constant stream of blood flowing from Steinberg's victims. I plucked up the courage and gulped as I pushed open the door in the hope that he would be too busy or that he would have a new assistant who knew a few more modern hairstyles. Alas, my hopes were dashed as I saw old Steinberg sitting in one of his black leather swivel chairs with his feet propped up in the neighbouring chair. He appeared to be reading the newspaper, but it was only when the bell tinkled as I entered that I realised he had been asleep. He snorted and scrumpled his paper.

"What did you say?" exclaimed Steinberg.

"Nothing," I answered, startled. "I've just arrived."

"Don't be cheeky to me, young man, or I'll have your guts for garters!" he continued, looking at me disdainfully as he stood in order to tower over me. He squinted one eye and cinched his mouth in tightly so that his lips resembled the rear end of Stephen's cat, Monty.

Steinberg rotated a chair wordlessly and gestured with his protruding chin for me to take a seat. I took off my coat and hung it on the coat stand before sitting and observing his preparations in the mirror. Doddering around behind me, he fetched a cape to put around my shoulders and stuffed a piece of kitchen roll down the back of my neck, nipping my neck as he did so.

"You nipped my neck!" I exclaimed.

"I never touched you," responded the old barber with his hand around the back of my neck.

Loose skin hung down off his jaw as if his face were melting; his eyes, sunken into the sockets of his skull, were bloodshot in the extreme. He had close-cropped, white hair around the back and sides of his own head with a smooth bald dome on top; it was almost certain that he had cut it himself. Although he had nothing in his mouth, he moved his jaw as if he were chewing something. Every now and then he parted his lips to reveal teeth that resembled mangled peanuts; he certainly would not have inspired confidence if he'd been a dentist. I could smell a mixture of strong odours in the shop; something like the TCP that Grandpa used for any graze, cough or other ailment was the overriding scent, but there were also sickly-sweet notes of aftershave lotion and more than a hint of whisky each time Steinberg came close to me. I knew it was whisky because my dad and Uncle Peter had been savouring a 'single malt' on Christmas Day and asked me if I'd like to taste it. I asked them why I'd want to drink something that smelled of cat urine and told them that I didn't want to put hairs on my chest thank you very much.

Great. So, the barber was old and doddery, could barely see and had either been drinking strong alcohol this morning or enough last night that it was still noticeable. This was not going to be a good day.

"Number two at the back and sides, is it?" asked Steinberg reaching for the electric clippers. This was the only piece of modern equipment he owned and he was proud of it.

"No. Number four please," I answered, watching as he ignored my request completely and began to shear the back of my skull with the only comb attachment he had: the number two. I tried to distract myself by scanning the products on his dusty shelves: Old Spice, Brut 33, Brylcreem, Jelly Cool Cat pomade, talcum powder, and wondered what they were, and if these particular bottles and pots were older than I was. Glancing back into the mirror, I groaned as I watched the amount of hair that was falling off me. I hadn't expected anything else, but the reality was still hard to witness, and I felt very sorry for myself. I could already picture the delight on the faces of the likes of Walker, Batesy and Ottilie. They wouldn't even need to think up any insults at the beginning of this term; Steinberg was in the process of making me the prize laughing stock of the school.

After a couple of minutes, he switched off the clippers and took up the scissors, examining my head. He had completed the short back and sides and was ready to tackle the top. I fought back a tear as he turned my head to the left and right, furrowing his brow and biting on his tongue as he scrutinised his handiwork as if he were an artist. I'd never seen my scalp so clearly, and I felt cold and exposed. He seemed to be measuring how high he'd gone up the sides, and I arched my eyebrows in surprise to see that my hair was very uneven. There were about four centimetres of almost bald head above my left ear but about five centimetres above my right! Steinberg replaced the scissors and sparked up the clippers again in an attempt to rectify this misalignment. However, he missed his aim again, taking off too much hair on the left-hand side so that I was wonky on the other side!

"Stop moving," ordered Steinberg, opening his eyes wide and blinking to try to focus better.

I was about to protest that I'd been keeping more still than a Buddhist monk, but I thought that might give him an idea as to how to finish off the haircut, so I said nothing. He measured the side that was slightly longer with his fingers and then placed his hand on my head before clipping alongside it, finally evening out the two sides to leave about eight centimetres of hair in a stripe down the middle of my head. I tried to look stoic as a tear slid down my left cheek. He switched to the scissors and clacked away at the thin thatch that remained. I'd never really contemplated the shape of my head before, but it was becoming clear that I was more of a peanut than a roundhead.

Steinberg gave me the final few snips, and at last, the torture was over. At least, I would be able to wait another six months before needing another haircut. He mumbled something about what a 'Bobby Dazzler' he'd given me before holding out his hand for payment, slurping back a dribble of saliva that was escaping at the corner of his wrinkled mouth. I handed over the money silently and looked despairingly into the tub of out-of-date lollipops that he offered me along with his brown-toothed grin. I couldn't bring myself to take one, so I headed for the door, grateful for the small mercy that I'd brought my hooded coat, which I pulled over my head to cover the damage as fully as possible.

As the doorbell tinkled behind me, I was so wrapped up in my thoughts about how to avoid being teased that I forgot to tread carefully on the slippery pavement. Planting my left foot, I could feel that I had lost my grip and my balance was teetering. I shot my right foot across in a desperate attempt to remain upright but set it down on exactly the same icy patch that had deceived my left, and I fell back onto my bottom, arms helicoptering above my head. A quick check let me know that I wasn't injured at all, and I couldn't see anyone down the street who might have witnessed my stumble. A smile grew on my face as I thought about how being able to laugh at myself was going to have to become second nature, and a little slip like this must have looked pretty funny. I was pulling myself carefully back to my feet when I felt the stinging slap of a snowball to the back of my head.

"Nice fall, Mr Tumble!" came a voice from behind me. I turned to see a pair of little boys behind me on the other side of the road. They were giggling away at me, but their smirks grew even larger as I stood and my hood fell down to reveal my new haircut.

"Haha! Nice haircut, haircut boy!" yelled one of the boys before they turned tail and disappeared around a corner. My pride was knocked, but that only lasted for a moment until I replaced my hood and plodded on homewards, allowing myself a smile. I had decided that the best way to cope with this situation would have to be to laugh at myself harder than everybody else would.

Chapter 12
Steinberged

"Hey, Neil. What are you up to?" asked Stephen as I stepped through his front door.

"My neck in trouble," I answered.

I'd decided to stop in to see Stephen to get some advice about my hair rather than going straight home after my visit to the barber's.

"Ah. In that case, you'd better come in," he said, steepling his fingers as if he were an expert on everything. "Do you want to leave your coat?" he suggested, indicating the coat rack and beckoning me to follow him upstairs.

"Okay, but before I do, you have to brace yourself," I warned.

"Let me guess. Your nanna made you a new Christmas jumper again?" enquired Stephen.

I thought it best just to lay bare the issue and wait for his advice. The reaction of my best friend would give me some indication of how everybody else would respond once I got back to school on Monday. Slowly, I unzipped the front of my coat and then lowered the hood.

"Woah! Neil! That's...severe, mate. Have you been Steinberged?" gasped Stephen.

"Yes," I groaned. "The Turkish barbers were fully booked, so I had no choice. Tell me the truth. It's okay, isn't it?"

"Well, yes...er perhaps...actually, no. It's pretty bad. You'll know how it feels to be ginger now," he said.

"Maybe I'll grow a beard and join the circus," I said solemnly.

As we were talking, I noticed that Stephen couldn't stop looking at my hair, and that was disconcerting.

"Actually, that's about one minute, and I'm used to it already," consoled Stephen after he'd given me the full survey. "You'll probably get a few looks and comments on the first day but it'll be fine after that. You've just got to get through Monday. Now come up to my room, and see if there are any Christmas presents you want to swap."

We scampered up to his room without crossing either of his parents. I knew Mike Prince, Stephen's dad, very well since he and my dad spent a lot of time together, and he would surely feel free to have a good laugh at my expense as soon as he saw me. His mum must have been in the kitchen as she often made the most amazing cakes at the weekends, and I could smell something incredible wafting through the door. Stephen had fairly 'hands off' parents in comparison with mine, and he came and went as he pleased in general. He closed the door behind us in his room and ushered me over to his desk where his Christmas presents were.

"You can't have this one," he said pointing at a 'Hollyoaks Babes' calendar. As far as I knew, Stephen had never watched *Hollyoaks*, but he did seem very interested in the actresses in the show, particularly when they were wearing bikinis. I flipped through it without paying attention and then scanned the rest of his stash. He'd got some Lego sets, one of which he was in the middle of building. Stephen was a master builder and had got his dad to put up head-height shelving all around his bedroom for displaying the finished creations. We quickly worked out that we didn't have any Christmas present swapsies. Unsurprisingly, he didn't want my 'Jesus loves you' tapestry, and I didn't want his days of the week socks or the shower gel that he'd received. He'd also got a voice changer, but his was an Iron Man, one with glowing eyes, so we vowed to have some Iron Man versus Darth Vader quote wars in the coming weeks.

*

There was still a little snow, ice and slush on the ground as I waited at the school bus stop with Stephen, Grub and Cameron on the first Monday of the new school term. Anxiety about people's reaction to my haircut had prevented me from sleeping very well, and so I was particularly tired this morning with adrenaline keeping me going. I'd decided to put my hood down right from the start rather than revealing my new look later; that way people could see that I was comfortable and were less likely to mock. That was my theory. Grub had been worried that I might draw unwanted attention to our group, but Cameron said that I looked like a distinguished human rather than being just like everybody else.

I heard the phrase "He lost a fight with the lawnmower" from behind my back, accompanied by some chuckling but chose to ignore it and keep chatting with my friends. Cameron was a top skateboarder and had got a new skateboard for Christmas as well as a Darth Vader cape and lightsaber set. Grub had a remarkable singing voice for someone with relatively small lungs, and he had got a karaoke set and some coloured disco lights as his main presents. We were just arranging when would be a good time to go to his house to try out his new kit when Basher Walker and his sidekick Batesy ambled into view.

"Well, well. Fat Gollum has had his head skinned into a Sissy Melissy," appraised Walker. "Who knew that you were hiding a peanut under there?"

"Yeah," sniggered Batesy. "Nice Barnet, slap head."

I was expecting this and so laughed off their insults.

"I'm glad you like it. I'll give you the barber's address if you want the same."

"No, no. You don't get it," replied Walker, advancing slowly towards me. "You look even more like a mug than usual, and we don't want mugs sharing the bus with us."

As he was speaking, I could see out of the corner of my eye that Lemony had arrived at the bus stop but was nonchalantly ignoring the fact that I was being threatened. This was becoming another situation, and Stephen and

Cameron stood firm at my sides with Grub cowering just behind.

"I'd rather not share the bus with you either," I answered, "but some things are beyond our control."

"Aren't you listening to me?" threatened Walker, giving me a little tap on the side of the head. "I said…"

Walker drew back his hand to give me a harder slap across the side of the head when suddenly a bigger hand grasped his arm. His eyes filled with anger as he turned around but had to change the angle of his head to look upwards into the eyes of an unexpected intervener, Shaun Bush, our neighbour. He was an older boy, in the year above Lemony, and usually, his sort would ignore any little spats among the younger pupils, but he'd chosen to step in this time. All of the bravado melted away from Walker's angry features, and he now looked afraid, as if he was expecting a thump himself from Shaun who had almost proper man-muscles and had probably started shaving too.

"Piss off, Walker, you little turd," warned Shaun. "And don't mention his hair again, or I'll smash your face in."

"O-Okay," stammered Walker.

Shaun released his grip on Walker's arm, and the defeated bully stuffed his hands into his pockets and stomped away to wait for the bus further along from us. Batesy duly scampered after him. Walker glanced back over towards me, looking dejected, and I'll admit that I found his expression very satisfying: as satisfying as loosening a bit of food that's been trapped between your teeth for a long time or as satisfying as a particularly satisfying poo.

"Thanks," I said to Shaun.

He just nodded and shrugged, looking away from me immediately. I followed his gaze and saw that he was looking over to where Lemony was chatting with Ella, seemingly unaware of anything other than her conversation. I understood that Shaun had not stood up for me to fight against injustice or because he was my neighbour, but he did it hoping for Lemony's approval. He had lived next door to us for years, but we had not really had much to do with the

Bushes. It seemed that Shaun had developed a crush on Lemony, and that was fine by me if he was going to be my guardian and keep Walker away from us.

The direction of Shaun's gaze hadn't escaped Stephen's attention either.

"Oh man," he said. "He saved you just to impress Lemony. I'm not surprised though."

"Here we go again," said Grub, as he and Cameron rolled their eyes.

"Well, Valentine's day is coming up soon," persisted Stephen. "Why would she go for someone who's older when she could have a needy, available, flame-haired, desperate younger man?"

"Be a good human and give it a rest, Stephen," suggested Cameron.

"You've got to admit it," Stephen added finally. "She is hot."

"Actually, no. Quite the opposite," I concluded. "She must be the coldest person I know."

The bus arrived.

*

My new haircut did attract a lot of looks and some snide comments on that first day back, but, as Stephen had said, everybody seemed to have got used to it by lunchtime, and the interest was waning. By the time we were into afternoon lessons, my lack of sleep from the night before was really beginning to catch up with me. We were coming towards the end of a Maths lesson, and Mr Campbell was wrapping up a summary about fractions and percentages. His voice was soothingly monotonous, and I was struggling to keep my eyes open.

"I'm sorry if I'm boring you, Master Peel," said Mr Campbell, pulling me back to reality. "Is there somewhere else you'd rather be?"

All of the other pupils in my Maths class turned to look at me.

"Oh yes, sir. I'd rather be in bed," I replied to the odd titter from the other pupils. "I slept really badly last night, and your voice was making me nod off."

"Well, really, Master Peel," he said, recoiling in shock at my boldness. "How dare you…"

"Oh, sir. I do like Maths," I answered, just as the bell rang for the end of the day. "Honestly."

"Stay behind a moment, would you, Master Peel," he said sternly. "The rest of you can pack up, and we'll see how much you can remember about fractions next time."

Stephen grasped my shoulder on the way past me.

"Good luck, mate," he whispered.

Ottilie Plank sniggered with her friend, Remi as they left the classroom, and soon enough, I was left alone with Mr Campbell. I'd got through about half of the school year without too much trouble with the teachers but was worried that this was going to be my first proper reprimand.

"Well, then, Master Peel," he began. "Can you think of any reason why I shouldn't give you a thorough scolding?"

I couldn't believe what I was hearing!

"No, sir! Please don't pour boiling water over me!" I begged. "I won't be tired in your lessons again. I promise."

"Back up there a moment, Master Peel," he continued, calmly. "I said *scolding*, not *scalding*."

I wasn't entirely sure what scolding was, but it had to be better than scalding, so I was momentarily relieved.

"You may have noticed my haircut, sir," I explained. "I didn't ask the barber for this style, and I was very worried about how everyone else would react, so I barely got any sleep last night. I almost made it to the end of the day, but the lack of sleep caught up with me, I'm afraid. I do like your lessons and I wouldn't say it if it wasn't true; it's just that I got Steinberged."

Mr Campbell's face had been softening, but as I finished speaking, he tensed and sat up in his chair.

"Steinberged?" he inquired. "Steinberg, the barber in Lower Piercing?"

101

"Yes, sir," I replied, curious as to why Mr Campbell was so interested in our village barber.

"Steinberg…Steinberg," he repeated quietly, now staring out of the window. Eventually, he turned back to face me, although he was looking right through me as he spoke, as if looking back in time. "I've been teaching at this school for 12 years now, Master Peel, but I'll never forget my first day. I, too, went to Mr Steinberg's barbershop just before term began, and he gave me an awful haircut, much worse than yours, I might add. I used to wear my hair back, but he cut it so short at the front that I had a ridiculously short fringe. The pupils didn't dare tease me to my face, but I could tell that they were laughing about me behind my back. They had a nickname for me, which I don't care to share with you. I understand your pain; you are free to go, and we'll say no more about today's lesson."

I was surprised at his confession, but it made me realise that teachers were human too.

"Goodbye, sir," I said as I picked up my things to leave.

"Goodbye, Neil," he replied, but as I turned around, I saw that he had turned to face the window.

As I left the classroom and walked down the corridor, I realised that that was the first time I had ever heard him use a pupil's first name.

Chapter 13
Dad's Phone Call Disaster

One Friday evening in early February, I was doing my homework to get it out of the way, so that I could meet up with the boys on Saturday with a clear conscience. I'd nearly finished but was a bit stuck on a science question about the conditions necessary to make hydrogen explode. It reminded me of the time when Stephen had tried to set light to his farts and ended up singeing his scrotum before he got to prove his theory that he could produce a foot-long flame. Grub had been dispatched to fetch ice cubes.

I headed downstairs into the lounge with my exercise book in my hand and a quizzical look on my face. Asking for help here was probably not wise because Mum and Lemony were busy watching their favourite programme, *Victor Delta*, a police show about a handsome, witty detective who wasn't called Victor at all; he was called Peregrine. Every week he'd save the day in the face of adversity, and Mum would swoon.

Peregrine's boss, who was also not called Victor, seemed to be giving him a particularly hard time this week.

"I need results, goddamn it, Perry," he shouted. "What have you got for me?"

"A cheese sandwich," quipped Dad in reply from behind me. He had wandered into the lounge and was distractedly searching for something.

"Be quiet, John!" chided Mum. "We're trying to watch this."

"He's only jealous," added Lemony, "because he doesn't look like that."

"Me? Jealous?" snorted Dad. "You must be joking. Tall, dark and handsome with dimpled cheeks and sculpted abs is okay if you like that sort of thing. I tell you, Lemony, you should aim for someone medium height with salt and pepper hair and a slight potbelly. You'd have a much better chance of achieving your goal. That sort's a keeper. Just ask your Mum."

"John! For God's sake!" cried Mum, not taking her eyes off the television.

Dad went back to checking behind ornaments and underneath cushions as I became temporarily distracted by the events on the television.

"The minister's daughter's been missing for 24 hours already," insisted not-Victor, the police chief, "and what are you doing about it besides scratching your arse?"

"Well," replied Peregrine, straightening his tie with a sly look, "I've been pumping the minister's wife for information, of course."

Dad missed that one due to the fact that his head was behind the curtains.

"Has anybody seen my memory stick?" he asked, his voice muffled by the material.

"Here. Take mine," replied my irritated Mum, holding up a nail file.

Dad and I looked at each other, puzzled.

"I said memory stick, not emery stick," chuckled Dad. "You know, my USB?"

"No! Shhh!" answered Mum.

"Does anyone know what conditions you need to make Hydrogen explode?" I asked.

"I'm bloody well about to explode if I can't get some peace and quiet!" yelled Mum as Lemony shot me a typically acidic glance.

"Now get out of here and don't come back until you've got some answers for yourself," shouted not-Victor, the police chief, as if his conversation with the dreamy Peregrine had merged with ours.

I thought it would be safer to retreat for now and have another look at the question myself. I scratched my head over my homework for a few more minutes before realising that I hadn't actually asked Dad for help properly in my scramble to escape Mum's anger. Once again, I took up my book and tiptoed downstairs so as not to disturb the viewers. I had it in mind to play-act creeping over to Dad in mutual agreement about keeping the noise down, however, he wasn't in the kitchen. The back door was open, and I could hear Dad's voice. It was dark at this time of night, so he was most likely talking on the phone, but I wasn't sure why he would be taking a call outside. I wandered over to the door and listened for a moment to check if this sounded as if it was going to be a long call, meaning I'd have to try again for help later. He was speaking quietly, so I had to strain to hear.

"It's just I love you. Simple as that."

What!? My hand, which had been reaching for the back door handle, started trembling, and I suddenly felt as if I needed the toilet. Or rather, perhaps I was going to be sick. Or maybe both. My head started throbbing, and I was no longer aware of standing in the kitchen. Hundreds of thoughts flooded through my brain, thoughts that I had never had before about my parents.

"No. I know," continued Dad in a whisper. "I hate all of this sneaking around too, but we won't have to keep the secret much longer. I'll find a reason to slip out tomorrow. I've got to see you. Hold on. I think I heard something. It could be Emma. I've got to go, Diana."

I'd already backed out into the hallway, glad that I only had socks on my feet so that I could hurry silently up the stairs. I locked myself in the bathroom and sat on the toilet for a while. What was happening? Was my dad in love with another woman called Diana? There were a few children I knew whose parents were divorced, but that wasn't supposed to happen to me. I loved my dad. He was a good man. He loved my mum, didn't he? I was sure he did, or was that just what I wanted to think?

I got up and looked at myself in the mirror to see that I was really red in the face. I didn't think I'd been crying, but there was a tear track down my right cheek. My life had had its ups and downs, but it looked like it was going to take a dramatic turn now. What should I do? Was it better to confront Dad first or tell Mum what I'd overheard? I wanted to talk to Stephen about this. He'd probably tell me to ditch my honesty policy for something as big as this, but that wasn't going to happen. I couldn't bury my head in the sand and hope that this would all go away. It would torture me daily if I had to wait until Dad slipped up properly or Mum found out by accident. No. Swift action was needed. The consequences could be terrible, but they'd have to be faced sooner or later.

I let myself out of the bathroom and went straight to my room, closing the door behind me and changing into my pyjamas. As a little boy, I used to pull the duvet over my head to protect me. Monsters were very unlikely to be able to get through such a barrier, especially if the covers happened to be blue; monsters can't stand blue, as everybody knows. I turned off the light and covered myself completely as I used to do.

Stephen and I had running jokes that a friend in need is a pest, and that a problem shared is a problem doubled, but they didn't seem funny now. We would say that, but both of us would have done anything for the other one, and I needed a friend now. Family is supposed to be the one constant thing in life, but that crutch was about to be kicked away from under me. My friend's advice would be crucial in my strategy.

*

I seemed to have been in bed, but not asleep, for quite some time when there was a soft knock at the door and Dad opened it. Up until this moment, that would have been a completely normal occurrence, but this evening, I was left to contemplate the man who had been a rock in my life, crumbling to dust in my opinion before my eyes. How could he have done this to Mum and to us?

"There you are, Neil," whispered my treacherous father. "We thought you were still working. You didn't say goodnight. Are you feeling okay?"

"Not really, Dad," I answered, sitting up. I found I could barely look at him. I wondered how I felt about him now.

"What's up, me old pal?" he asked in a jolly tone.

Suddenly, my plan to discuss the situation sensibly with Stephen flew out of the window, and I blurted out my discovery.

"I know what you've been up to, Dad! I heard you on the phone outside earlier."

"What?" replied Dad, sounding perturbed. I could see from his silhouette that he was looking nervously from side to side. He continued in a whisper, easing his way into my room and switching on the light so that I was temporarily blinded. "Okay. Let's talk about this, but you've got to stay calm."

"Dad!" I cried.

"What's going on?" came Mum's voice from the foot of the stairs. "Is everyone okay? Is he up there, John? What's the shouting for?"

"Yes, love," called Dad through the crack in the doorway. "Err. He's in his room. We're just having a chat."

He then turned to me and spoke urgently in a hushed tone as we could hear Mum's footsteps climbing the stairs.

"Look, Neil. You understand that you can't tell Mum what you heard. It'll spoil everything. Please don't. Just let her find out later."

"What's going on?" asked Mum, who had appeared at Dad's shoulder. "Are you all right, sweetheart?"

"Dad's in love with a woman called Diana! I heard him on the phone earlier. He's sneaking out to see her tomorrow."

"What?" asked Mum, looking stunned and turning to look quizzically at Dad.

"No. Hold on a minute," stumbled Dad. "He's just confused. Let me have a chat with him."

"No. Are you saying that Neil's lying? Were you on the phone to someone else?"

"Well, yes. I was," said Dad, "but it wasn't…"

"Was it Diana Prince?" interrupted Mum.

Gut punch. I wasn't ready for that. Stephen's mum? I'd always called her Mrs Prince. I suppose I knew that her name was Diana, but it hadn't struck me that Dad was having an affair with Stephen's mother. Did that make it worse or better?

"Look. Okay, I was talking to Diana Prince but you're not letting me…" explained Dad before Mum stormed past him into their bedroom and slammed the door.

"Oh. Nice one, Neil!" shouted Dad, flushed in the face and clenching his fists in frustration while following Mum. "Look, Emma. I can explain everything."

I couldn't believe that he was blaming me for this. I got out of bed and walked over to the doorway. My heart was racing at the scene. My parents had never really argued much, and so this was a new extreme. Dad was leaning against the door, knocking and calling Mum's name. Just then, Lemony came up the stairs.

"What's all the shouting for?" she said calmly. "I found your memory stick, Dad. You left it in the computer, you numpty."

"Aha! Evidence," cried Dad, ecstatically, grabbing the USB and kissing Lemony. "Emma. Please open the door, and let me explain. I promise I'm not having an affair."

"Woah. That escalated quickly," said Lemony, grinning. "I want to hear this."

I was surprised that she didn't seem too worried that her parents' marriage was in jeopardy, but then I'm not sure what it would take to unnerve my sister. Mum opened the bedroom door.

"You've got sixty seconds before I pack a bag and head to my Sue's," she said sternly.

"Okay. Here goes," started Dad. "It's Valentine's day next week, so I'd asked Diana to make a heart-shaped cake for you. I would have made it myself, but I haven't got the mould, and I'd probably have ruined it. I drew the design at work, scanned it and was supposed to send her over the picture to copy, but I couldn't find my memory stick, so I described it to her on the phone. Neil must have heard me telling her to write 'I love you' in icing on the top. I couldn't send her the picture, so I was going to pop around and take my drawing tomorrow. It was going to be a surprise."

Mum stood silently, not knowing what to think. Eventually, it was Lemony who spoke.

"You should believe him, Mum. I looked on the memory stick, and there is indeed a scan of a crappy drawing of a heart-shaped cake with 'I love you' written on it. Since we're spoiling surprises tonight, you might also get something special from Knaughty Knickers dot com, judging by the receipt that's saved on the USB. Something I wish I hadn't seen. Gross one, Father. Well. That's enough excitement for Lemony. I'm off to bed. Good night all."

With that, she went into her room and closed the door.

Within two minutes, Lemony had undone the harm that I had caused and returned our family life to normality. I reran the conversation I'd overheard between Dad and Mrs Prince before coming to the conclusion that everything seemed to match what Dad was claiming. It took us a while to calm down, but Mum and Dad hugged, Mum saying that the gesture was lovely, and that we'd probably laugh about this once the emotions had died down. Dad seemed to forgive me for spoiling his surprise, giving me a pretend box around the ears before kissing me good night.

As I lay in bed, I reflected on the evening's drama, trying to decide whether honesty had been the best choice today. I concluded that it had. Dad's surprise may have been spoilt, but at least I wouldn't have had to carry a burden of worries around with me until Valentine's day. After another hour, my heart rate had slowed down enough that I could get to sleep.

Chapter 14
What We Heard in the Woods

Before long, the Easter holidays were upon us, and we were desperate to get back to our Dungeons and Dragons game. It had been on a hiatus for too long, but you need a good chunk of time to play these things, and our Christmas holiday had been too short. We decided to get Cameron fully involved in the game, but he had never played before, so we had to explain a lot of rules and conventions to him. Three adventurers, however, offered much greater chances of success than just two, and since we had magic and dexterity covered with Stephen's Archmage and my Half-elf, we thought that some brute strength wouldn't go amiss; Cameron would play a barbarian warrior.

Cameron's great grandmother wasn't very well, and so his parents were spending a lot of time looking after her. That meant that he was able to come around to my house and solve their dilemma of who would look after him. The first time that we sat around the dining table and got out our manuals and character sheets, I was puzzled to see that I barely recognised my Half-elf at all. Chewing on a room-temperature cross bun, I frowned in confusion at the details before my eyes. I was sure that his name had been Hendel and not Geoffrey Pantsniffer. I'd exchanged some of my gold pieces for potions and items, but I remembered them as potions of healing and strength rather than a potion of unexplained custard and *portion* of turnip. Furthermore, my light sword was rubbed out and limp celery had been written in its place while my longbow had been replaced by a pea shooter. Where I'd had thirty-five remaining gold coins, there was now an IOU for 500 gold pieces and all of my skills of strength, dexterity, constitution, wisdom and intelligence were down to minus five; where my charisma score should have been was written 'n/a'.

I thought I had filled in the Features and Traits box with information that Hendel was a quiet, brooding and nimble fellow, but the description before me read as follows:

Geoffrey is a limp-wristed elf who was neutered by his best friend after a dispute about who could pee the furthest. As his name suggests, he particularly enjoys sniffing pants, especially when his victim is still wearing them. He usually exclaims "Ah Bisto!" to announce the presence of his face at someone's nether regions, although he has no element of surprise because you can smell him a mile away, such is his stench. He is a scrawny little shrieker and a disgrace to all other elves. In fact, he was kicked out of Elfville for cracking out a particularly loud, eggy fart during a sacred tree-hugging ceremony. He is likely to run away from any enemy, probably wetting his pants, plus he is a vegetarian. His greatest skill is that he is quite aerodynamic (when falling over) due to the fact that he tucks his glistening, yeasty chode away most fiercely to avoid wind resistance.

"What's a chode?" I asked.

"Dunno," muttered Stephen, not looking up from his character sheet.

Grub glanced at me and then flicked through his creature manual in search of this mystery beast.

Just then, Lemony sauntered in towards the bin with an empty crisp packet in her hand. She was chuckling to herself, and she turned towards us as the bin snapped shut.

"Have you only just discovered that?" she asked. "I updated your character so long ago that I'd forgotten I'd done it. I think it was even before Christmas. You should play him as I left him. The game would be far more fun."

"Lemony!" I bellowed. "If I went into your things, you'd go mental. Why don't you just leave my stuff alone if you say you don't care about me?"

She shook her head, snickering again as she glided out of the room and back upstairs.

"Humans," reflected Cameron, ponderously.

I showed the boys Geoffrey Pantsniffer's statistics, and their laughter eventually convinced me that, although it was very annoying, Lemony's prank was *quite* funny. I could still see my original pencil marks underneath her amendments, so, as I altered the weedy Geoffrey back into Hendel, I reflected that this was at least better than when she had previously interfered. That time, I had been the dungeon master, Stephen and Grub the intrepid adventurers, and they had just slain Pogmansi, the final Necromancer. Turning the page to deliver the end of the story and the victory spoils, I found that the quest resolution pages had been neatly removed. Lemony had denied it, but it couldn't have been anybody else.

Lemony held some sort of power over my parents, and so they never really told her off for her mischief. I think that they knew she was so temperamental and indifferent that if they reprimanded her properly, they could turn her against them for good. She was getting older and would not need them for much longer, so they were hanging on to the relationship that remained. She, of course, knew this and exploited the situation so that she could do pretty much as she pleased, and we all had to accept it.

Her changes to my Dungeons and Dragons character, however, were very minor and I had soon forgotten them. We played just about every day of the Easter holidays except one when Cameron had to go to see his great-grandma. It seemed that she wasn't going to live much longer, so it was probably a goodbye visit. Grub, Stephen and I still met up though and headed down to our tree by the river. Cameron had become such a familiar part of our group that it almost seemed odd to be back to our 'spectacular threesome'; I was now used to a 'fabulous foursome' but it was still a great feeling of freedom to be carefree with good friends.

*

The holidays did not last long enough, and the summer term started too soon. At Titfield, I now felt as if I was part of the school rather than just a new boy. Shaun Bush still had a crush on Lemony, and she still studiously ignored him. Thankfully, he was proving to be persistent, and so Walker and Batesy steered clear of us at the bus stop, not wanting to suffer any further humiliation at the hands of an older boy. This was, of course, perfectly fine by me.

One beautiful Wednesday in May, just after we had finished school, we were all waiting for the bus. We waited and waited but twenty minutes after we should have departed Mrs Deanus came trotting over towards us to tell us that our bus had broken down, and the company couldn't send out a replacement.

"Apparently, the driver had changed into reverse gear, and the knob got stuck, so he can only drive backwards," explained Mrs Deanus, chuckling to the disappointed, assembled would-be passengers.

"My dad always uses his hand to change gear rather than his knob," whispered Stephen to make us all laugh.

We could have gone back to the school office to call our parents, but mine certainly wouldn't have finished work for at least another hour, and Stephen, Grub and Cameron were in the same boat. The rest of the unfortunate bus passengers were making their own decisions and heading off in different directions. We were contemplating walking back since it was such a glorious day. It would be about an hour's walk, but it would be light for a long time yet, so I went over to let Lemony know my plans.

"We're going to walk back through the woods," I said.

"Oh good," she replied, turning slightly towards me but still not really taking her focus away from her friend, Ella. "You could do with the exercise."

113

"I get plenty of exercise," I retorted.

"Then why are you still fat?"

Ella giggled as I turned away, wondering why I'd even bothered to let my sister know.

The route back took quite a while, but it really was scenic. Late spring or early summer, depending on your viewpoint, was a lovely time to be outdoors: trees bloomed, birds sang, insects buzzed around busily. I suppose I was quite a fan of all nature. Except for wasps. And mosquitos. And ants. Oh, and those clouds of midges that get in your eyes or mouth when you walk through them and they get stuck in your throat, so you have to swallow them or try to hack them back up. Houseflies were pretty pesky too; they kept laying eggs in our food recycling, and those hatched into maggots, which made the wheelie bin stink.

Only the beginning and end of our journey were in built-up areas; the main part was along public footpaths and through the vast Badby woods. We used to go there as a family in autumn when I was younger, and the stunning reds and oranges of the leaves remain in my memory. It looked different now as everything was a lush green, but it was still beautiful.

Stephen was lamenting that, even though it was only two days until the summer half-term break, he wasn't going to be around for the first Saturday.

"We're going to my uncle and auntie's house," he explained. "Apparently, my uncle got tickets to a cricket match, and my mum volunteered me to go with him. I mean, she must know that I don't know what it's all about, and I've got no interest in cricket, but she said '*Oh, Stephen will go with you*' without even batting an eyelid."

"Good. That would have been very painful," I replied.

"What are you talking about?" asked Stephen, perplexed.

"Well, I don't know that much about cricket either, but 'batting an eyelid' sounds very painful as does 'bowling your googlies'. You're much safer avoiding dangerous sports like that," I suggested.

Grub reached for his glasses protectively at the thought of a cricket bat approaching his eyelids. "Actually," he said, seeming confident, "I know all about cricket. My dad was always watching it, so I asked him to explain it to me. It's quite easy really. First of all, everyone puts their stumps up to see who goes first. Then only one person can move at a time. Tombola throws the ball sidewise windmill style at Batman who has to hit it as high in the air as possible. He then has to run six around the court before one of the fieldy men catches it. You do this six times, and then it's over, but that doesn't mean that it's the end. If someone throws it on the leg side, then you're LGBTW, which means that you're out. If this happens, or you slip, then you can go in for tea and sandwiches."

"Hang on," said Stephen, looking puzzled. "If you're out, you go in? That doesn't make sense."

"Well, that's how it works," continued Grub. "Oh. Also, you have to put a plastic thing in your pants to protect big Jim and the twins because they try to throw the ball at your googlies. It looks like a nose protector, but you shouldn't put it on your face, especially if it's a shared one. You can't stand too close because Dad says that's silly. Finally, the game has to last at least six hours or else it's just not cricket."

"What would it be if it finished early?" asked Cameron who was clearly impressed by Grub's superior sporting knowledge.

"I'm not sure about that," answered Grub. "Croquet perhaps?"

"It sounds pretty confusing to me," I added, none the wiser.

"Six hours?" moaned Stephen. "I'd rather snog Ottilie Plank than suffer that."

Just then we heard a noise up ahead and off the main footpath. It sounded like a shriek of terror, so we stood in silence for a moment before I beckoned the others to follow me. Grub grabbed at my arm to hold me back.

"Let's just keep going," he whispered. "If this was a 'choose your own adventure' book, and we could go east or west, then west is the way that my specs get broken. You can't keep your finger in the page and go back in real life, and these are expensive glasses. They're from a prescription you know, not just a two for one deal."

I shushed him and dragged him towards the noise. We approached stealthily, so as not to disturb whatever was going on. Crouching down behind a fallen tree, we watched as our classmate, Wilberforce Pudge, panted into view. He wasn't exactly running, but it was clear that he was being pursued. Sure enough, Basher Walker and Batesy jogged up behind him and cornered him. Since we had been off-limits to their bullying of late, they had turned their attention to an even easier target, and Wilberforce was a classic victim.

Walker grabbed him by the scruff of his collar and shoved him up against a tree. I was ready to step in again, but Stephen and Grub, who were either side of me, held me back to keep us hidden.

"Can I do him, Basher?" asked an excited Batesy.

"Nah. We're not gonna hurt our partner, are we?" explained Walker. "We've got a business proposition for you, fatty. This weekend, we're gonna do dead, old Mrs Jackson's house. We're gonna clean her out, and you, you fat slag, you're gonna help us do it."

Wilberforce protested that Mrs Jackson was a witch and that he didn't dare go into her house, even if she had recently died. After all, she did live on Broomstick Lane. He thought the body might still be inside the house. Walker and Batesy, however, swayed him by telling him they had a chocolate cake slice to whet his appetite and a tin of French fancies for when the job was done. All he had to do was turn up at eleven o'clock on Sunday night, outside Mrs Jackson's house, dressed in black.

"Now, be a good boy and do as we've said, or you'll get what's coming to you," threatened Walker, producing a sticky slice of cake and squashing it into Wilberforce's palm. He stood back, and then Batesy, who had grabbed a long stick from the ground, proceeded to crack the hapless victim across the back of the knees, so he dropped his cake on the ground. Again, I tried to move out to help, but the two bullies had had their fill; they laughed and jogged away, leaving Wilberforce red-faced.

Once the coast was clear, we all moved forward to check on the poor lad.

"We heard everything. Are you okay, Wilberforce?" I asked.

"I don't know," he replied. "I'm getting a bit sick of them, but I suppose I've got used to their teasing and the odd knock at school. This is different though. I'm not usually allowed out that late, especially if my parents don't know where I am, and Mrs Jackson was a witch, everyone says so, even if she is dead, she might be able to come back and get me and turn me into a mouse or something. But Walker and Batesy will only pull my arms out of their sockets and poke my eyes if I don't cooperate. I don't know what to do."

"She wasn't a witch," said Cameron quietly. "She was my great grandmother."

All of us turned to face him in surprise.

"She was actually a lovely lady, but she had been losing her sight, so she didn't go out much anymore. I suppose her house does look a little spooky, but I used to love playing hide and seek around it when I was younger. We're due to go over there next Tuesday to help move some of her stuff, but those two are aiming to get in before that. We can't let it happen. We should tell the police."

"I don't know about that," said Wilberforce, looking worried. "I don't think the police would do anything about something that *might* happen, and it would get me in even more trouble with those two."

"He's right," added Grub nervously. "No police."

"I agree," I said. "But we need to put a stop to this once and for all. You shouldn't have to get used to teasing and bashing at school, and there's no way they should be able to force you into committing a crime. We're going to make a plan and turn this around onto them. We have to make Walker and Batesy regret that they ever picked on us."

Chapter 15
Formulating Tactics

Wilberforce was sweating cobs, and he claimed his blood sugar level was low. He was, as he put it, *heading into the arena of the unwell*, so we decided to go to the café on the edge of the woods to talk about what we should do. Cameron had ten pounds that he hadn't spent at the tuck shop, and he volunteered it for the greater good. I felt very grown-up going into a café without a grown-up, and it seemed like a natural instinct to act nonchalantly older, as if going into cafés was something that we did all of the time. Ten pounds wasn't going to go as far as we'd first thought, so we ordered five glasses of tap water in order to afford a slice of cake each.

"There you go, boys," said waitress Doris cheerily as she placed our cake down on the table before scratching her bum and shuffling back towards the kitchen.

"So, what's the plan, Stan?" whispered Stephen, keeping his head low over the table to avoid being overheard.

"Teachers," proposed Grub assertively, tapping the table with his finger. "We should tell Mrs Deanus, and she'll know what to do."

"No," I insisted. "No teachers." I'd been thinking things through while walking from the woods to the café and had the beginnings of what I thought could be a good idea. "We're throwing the rule book in the bin, and we're going to do this ourselves."

"Yes!" said Stephen with excitement. "This is going to be textbook."

"Wait a minute," said a confused Grub. "I thought we were throwing the book in the bin."

"That was the rule book," answered Stephen. "This is the *Neil Peel* textbook. You've got a plan, haven't you, Neil."

"I've got an idea," I said. "But we've all got to be in, one hundred per cent, and we can't tell anyone else what we're doing. Are we in?"

"Hang on," stammered Grub, nervously. "Let's not jump before we can leap. What are you asking us to sign up for?"

Wilberforce had already finished his slice of cake and had picked up Grub's without even looking down. He was halfway through it, and he too was looking uneasy.

"I'm up for it, but give us the details to help convince these guys," said Stephen, spreading his arms to pat Grub and Wilberforce on the shoulders.

"Okay," I began, feeling as if I were a crime boss in a very serious television programme. "First of all, I need to know if you can get hold of the key to Mrs Jackson's house, Cameron."

"Yes," he replied. "It's hanging on our cup and key rack at home. It's really easy to spot because it has a black cat on the keyring."

This was a great relief for me as my plan would have backfired immediately if we couldn't get into the house. Wilberforce, however, looked a little spooked at the mention of a black cat on the fob, probably reverting to thinking that we were dealing with a witch rather than a deceased old granny.

"Great," I continued. "Now, I was thinking about all of the things that we got for Christmas and how we could combine them to set a trap. Wilberforce can turn up to meet Walker and Batesy, just as they've asked, but we'll rig the house beforehand. Cameron's Darth Vader cape and Stephen's Iron Man mask would work well together. It's got glowing eyes, and you can make some wicked-ass sounds through the voice changer mouthpiece. One of us can wear them and pretend to be a witch. I mean, I know she wasn't one, but they don't know that. Lemony had some yellow contact lenses for Hallowe'en, so I'll get them, and Wilberforce can put them in once he gets in the house. You'll have to say something like 'please don't send me in there to check if the coast is clear' so that they'll send you in there to check if the coast is clear. That should give you enough time to put the lenses in before we open the door and reveal the witch and the converted Wilberforce. We could set up Grub's coloured karaoke lights out of the way to make the atmosphere just right as well. Perhaps Cameron can skateboard past in some kind of long outfit as if he's a spooky minion or something."

I paused to let the idea sink in and gauge the reaction. Stephen looked doubtful.

"Well, I was behind you all the way until you told us the plan. I'm not saying I won't do it," he said, "but your scheme sounds like there are a few holes in it. I mean, Walker and Batesy are stupid, but are they stupid enough to believe that it's not just us messing around in a disguise and playing on a skateboard at a home disco?"

I'd pictured this as a masterpiece of creativity that couldn't fail, but Stephen was unsure.

"Anyone else can chip in with an idea too," I said, hopeful that our combined efforts would add flesh to the bones of my plan. "What's the house like on the inside, Cameron?"

"Well, the front door opens, and there's the lounge on the left and the dining room on your right. There aren't any doors inside, just what my dad calls open plan. One thing that could help is that Great Grandma had one of those stairlifts, and I used to think it looked like she was floating down the stairs because they run from above the dining room downwards, right to left, rather than directly towards the front door, so you can't see the lift. Perhaps you could start at the top of the stairs in your costume, Neil, and float down on the lift. That would look pretty cool."

At what point the main witch actor had become me, I wasn't sure, but nobody else seemed to be jumping in to claim the role. Just then Wilberforce spoke up, having finished Grub's cake as well as his own.

"If you wanted to add real atmosphere, then I've got a dry ice machine at home."

I turned to him and blinked in amazement. Looking around the table, I noticed that the others were doing the same; Stephen had even forgotten to close his mouth.

"My dad's a science teacher at the college in Lowcester, and he likes to encourage me to have science as a hobby. We've got a couple of massive containers of dry ice in our garage storage right now. He'd be delighted if I was staying with a friend, and I'm sure I could sneak it out if someone could pick me up. Friends are another thing he's trying to encourage."

The rest of us didn't quite know what to say at first. I was initially a bit ashamed that I had a good group of friends, and Wilberforce clearly did not. I had stood up for him in the past, but had I really done much to make sure he wasn't on his own? Not especially.

"Well that's a game-changer," said Stephen, who now looked much more positive.

"Yes," I said. "Dry ice elevates this from a flawed plan into something that might just work pretty well."

"My lights can be set to any colours. They're LEDs," added Grub. "I bet we can get a pretty cool effect on the smoke."

"And if I skateboard around and you can't see my feet then it'll look like I'm floating too," said Cameron, also looking more enthused now.

"I must say that this is a bizarre coincidence that you happen to have the very thing we need to make Neil's plan more potentially likely to succeed," pointed out Stephen to Wilberforce.

"That's true," he replied. "It's especially convenient that we've just got hold of the containers of dry ice, so it will still be fine for Sunday."

"Yes. What are the chances of that?" added Grub, pushing his glasses back up the bridge of his nose. "Probably about three thousand, seven hundred and twenty to one."

"Indeed," I said. "This is very good luck."

"Yes, it is," answered Wilberforce.

"Almost unimaginably good luck for this to happen to us right now," added Cameron.

"Yes," said Wilberforce.

"Yes," I said.

"Yes," said Wilberforce.

"I wasn't sure at first," said Stephen, "but now we've got some details, we're really crossing the 'I's and dotting the 'T's with this."

Grub crossed his eyes at Stephen's mistake and smiled.

We moved on excitedly to fine-tuning the details of who would go where and how we would convince our parents to let us out late on Sunday night or else whether we should just sneak out. After all, eleven o'clock was very late, and we would almost certainly be back after midnight. We all had a role to play, and even Wilberforce and Grub, the less courageous members of our team, seemed happy to take part.

Doris, the waitress, shuffled back over to our table, grinning condescendingly at us. Didn't she realise what geniuses she was lucky to be serving?

"Would you like to pay now, dears?" she asked.

"No. Not really," I answered. "Is it optional?"

Doris looked a little shocked, but Cameron pulled out his money, and we paid and left the café. There was a renewed spring in our stride as we continued our journey home. We were about to arrive in Lower Piercing, and something was still nagging at me about the plan. It was good, but there was something missing.

"I think the plan is good, but there's something missing," I announced. "I just think we need something else. Something to convince Walker that this really is supernatural so that he won't just be scared for a short time and then go back to picking on Wilberforce or us a week later."

We carried on walking for a few more paces before Cameron stopped still. The rest of us turned to see what he was doing. He was calm as usual and was looking downwards.

"Are you all right, mate?" asked Stephen.

Cameron raised his eyes towards us. His expression was difficult to read, but I think he was perhaps smiling a little.

"I've never told you why Walker leaves me alone and how I've been able to get him to stop him bothering people," he said quietly.

This was big. I could sense it. Cameron was our friend, but his manner was such that you felt uncomfortable asking him certain questions. He was the kind of boy who would let you know things when he thought you needed to know them. This seemed like one of those moments, so none of us said anything, allowing him to continue at his own pace.

"Well," he continued. "I've got something on him that nobody else knows. Not even his weaselly sidekick, I'd bet. I think we could use it on Sunday."

Cameron explained.

Chapter 16
Convincing My Parents

The next day was a strange mix of heightened senses and a foggy blur. I found myself checking the time frequently and going over all of the possible outcomes in my head, barely concentrating on my lessons. In fact, the only time I wasn't concentrating on our scheme was when Mr Lashley had got us doing chest passes with a netball in our PE lesson, and Grub asked me why the Lord's prayer told us to forgive those who 'chest pass' against us. I thought he'd made quite a good joke until I realised that he was asking a genuine question.

The clocks seemed to be moving backwards during lessons, but break times when the four of us (we were distanced from Wilberforce so as not to arouse suspicion) were able to discuss the matter were over in the blink of an eye.

It seemed that the other boys all had a scheme so that they would have no problems being out late on Sunday. Cameron had told his parents that he was going to give them some space by staying at Stephen's house. Grub had said he was going too because Cameron needed emotional support; how he was going to get his disco lights over was a different question. Stephen didn't need to say anything since his parents probably wouldn't bother checking on him anyway. Wilberforce's parents were delighted when he told them that he was having a sleepover with a friend, but his mother was concerned about it being his first time. He had pretended to be sad and said that he would cancel the arrangement, knowing that she would give in and agree to his going.

The only one with a problem was me. The others had all lied to their parents, but I couldn't do that. In almost all previous situations, telling the truth had been a good idea in the long run, but this time, it could mean that I would be kept in, and the whole plan could fail.

While sitting around the dinner table on Thursday evening, I was contemplating not saying anything at all and just sneaking out of the house on Sunday night. That was a risky proposition because if I got caught, I'd be in trouble, and the others would be up the creek. In addition, we had the issue of how to get Wilberforce's dry ice machine over to Mrs Jackson's house.

Mum must have noticed that I was distractedly flicking a loose pea up against the mound of mashed potato on my cottage pie, as if it were a football.

"Goal!" she said. "Are you all right, Neil? Have you got something on your mind?"

Her tone was concerned, so I decided that now was the right time.

"There's a boy in my class who gets bullied all of the time," I began, looking from Mum to Dad and back again. Lemony carried on eating, but Mum and Dad both seemed to be paying attention.

"Basher Walker and Batesy make his life a living hell, and they're even trying to get him to commit a crime with them."

"Oh, that sounds awful!" replied Mum.

"It is," I continued, "and so I've decided to put a stop to it."

"Good for you, Neil," said Dad. "Walker? Is that the bully you told me about months ago?"

"Yes," I answered.

"Standing up for those who can't stand up for themselves is really commendable, but don't do anything dangerous, will you?" said Dad.

"What are you going to do?" asked Mum. "Tell Mrs Deanus about it?"

"No," I replied, gathering myself to lay my cards on the table. "That wouldn't stop them for five minutes. We've got to do something bigger than that, so I came up with a plan, and I want you to trust me and also to help me with it."

I noticed that Lemony has slowed her chewing down so that I could tell she was intrigued, even though she wasn't looking at me. I explained that I would need to go out until late on Sunday night, that I'd need Dad to drive me over to collect Wilberforce and his kit and probably Grub and his lights too before dropping us off at Broomstick Lane. We weren't doing anything illegal, and there would be five of us and two of them. We only planned to scare them, but even if we failed, we still shouldn't be in physical danger.

"I don't know about that," said Mum, looking concerned. "What do you think, John?"

"We have to do it, Mum," I said calmly. "Or else they'll just keep on bullying that poor boy. You have to believe me that it's the truth, and it's not that I want to do this so much as that I have to."

I realised that I was playing up the fact that this was the only way to protect the weak and uphold justice, but it seemed to be working. Mum and Dad exchanged glances and even Lemony looked up at them, waiting for their answer.

"Okay," said Dad, finally. "I'll help you. We have to believe what you've said, and if it works, then you'll have done something pretty heroic for that young lad."

Mum looked anxiously across at Dad. I think she might have been hoping that he'd say no so that she didn't have to be the bad guy. After a short pause, she nodded her head in resigned agreement.

"But be careful," she said.

"Oh, and there's one other thing," I said, turning to Lemony. "Could we borrow your yellow contact lenses please?"

*

127

When the bell rang for the end of school on Friday, I realised that I hadn't learned a single thing all day; I'd been so preoccupied with what lay ahead. It was fortunate that no teachers had asked me any difficult questions, or else I might have undone the plan if they'd asked me what was distracting me. I replayed the look on Lemony's face from last night's dinner. It had been difficult to read. At first, I thought she was angry that I'd put her on the spot by asking for her contact lenses straight after Mum and Dad had agreed to help me, as she could hardly say no. She'd clenched her jaw in a way that was either a hidden smile or gritted teeth before consenting. Was she proud of what I was doing or perhaps annoyed that I was up to the kind of mischief that she enjoyed so much?

It was terribly difficult not to look at Wilberforce but also not to look like we weren't looking at him during our bus journey home. Walker and Batesy kept glancing over towards him, and Wilberforce looked back nervously. They took him aside once we'd all got off the bus and had a quiet chat together before separating and heading off home.

Cameron, Grub, Stephen and I talked through our final checklists as we made our way home from the bus stop. We were good to go for Sunday.

As soon as I got home, I ran upstairs and rechecked all of the necessary items I'd laid out the day before. My costume and mask, check. Contact lenses, check. Everything was prepared, but I still had butterflies in my stomach.

Chapter 17
Training Day

My alarm rang at seven o'clock, and I rubbed my eyes, wondering what was happening. I was still tired and had that Saturday morning feeling which meant that there was no need for me to get up, so why had the alarm gone off? Had I forgotten to change it? Then it struck me.

TRAINING DAY!

I had big responsibilities coming up with our operation on Sunday night, and I would have to be sharp: at the top of my game (whatever that meant). I had to admit that fitness has never been high on my priority list, but lately, it had slid way too far down, and I was softer around the middle than usual. I intended to be a lean machine, toned and ready for action.

What I needed was a training regime, and today was the first day.

I dropped to the floor, adopting the sit-up position with my feet wedged underneath the bed and hands behind my head. A quick fifty should get me started. You can't overdo this sort of thing when you're not in the habit, but I wanted to feel the burn. Just as I was about to start sit-up number one, I realised that I needed to go for a number one, and I was already feeling the burn in my bladder. Okay. Toilet first, then exercise.

The first pee of the day was sweet relief. Urine, 'ur-out'. I flushed and then headed back towards my room until I remembered that hydration was crucial. All the fitness gurus swore that you shouldn't begin exercise if you were dehydrated, so I turned around and headed downstairs to the kitchen and filled a glass with water. Having drained that, I mentally ticked off phase one of the programme: this was going very well indeed!

Before heading back upstairs, I heard a low rumble from my stomach and then glanced at the fridge thinking about nutrition. Rocky Balboa had raw eggs for breakfast, and he had the kind of shape I hoped to be in by this evening; if it was good enough for Rocky, it was good enough for me. We had three eggs left, and that would be perfect. Not being an expert at cracking eggs, it took me about ten minutes to remove all of the little bits of shell from my glass; the white is very sticky, especially those 'snotty bits', as Lemony calls them, that join the white to the yolk.

I was just opening the kitchen drawer and reaching for a fork to beat the eggs when Mum's voice interrupted me.

"What are you doing up, love? It's not even half-past seven, and it's Saturday."

She gave one of her 'oi, oi, oi' yawns while pulling the cord of her fluffy, pink dressing cord tight around her waist.

"Protein, Mum," I replied. "An athlete's diet is all about protein, and this is a perfect source to start the day. You can't get the body of a Greek God by lazing in bed on a Saturday morning, can you?"

"I suppose not, but I need those eggs," she protested, half-smiling at my analogy. "I was going to make a chocolate cake this morning, and I really don't want to have to go to the shops again just for eggs. Can't you have toast or cereal?"

This was a conundrum, but Mum did make exceedingly good chocolate cakes, so I handed over the egg glass and went to the food cupboard.

"Okay. Brown bread should still be fine. That's got lots of fibre in it."

"Sorry, darling. We've only got white. Anyway, what's with the 'athlete's diet'? Are you feeling all right? Is this anything to with tomorrow night?" she asked, looking concerned.

"Mother, this is the new me, so you might as well get used to it."

I was keen not to let the full details of our plans slip, but none of what I was saying was a lie. I took out the white bread and decided on three slices. After all, I was going to need a lot of energy with all of the activity I was going to be doing today. They had to be buttered, of course, since who eats dry toast? A moron, that's who. The selection of spreads was quite wide, but my eyes settled on the jar of supermarket's own brand hazelnut spread. Nuts had protein in them, and a quick check told me that there were 6.3 grammes per hundred, so that sounded like a good substitute for my eggs. There were some statistics about saturated fats and sugars too, but I was focusing on the protein. Yummy!

I licked the last of the chocolatey spread from the edges of my mouth and left my plate by the sink; miraculously, the plates always seemed to find their way into the dishwasher without my help, although I have to admit to putting them in badly on purpose, in places where Dad would always stack cups, so that I would be told 'oh, just leave it to me'.

Right. Back up to my room to get ready for my active day. All the suckers were still in their beds while I was like a pale, young, chubby Mo Farah. I'd figured a 5km jog would be a good light warm-up. As a novice runner, I'd allowed fifteen minutes for that as it was probably only down to the park and back. A quick rifle through my drawers provided an older T-shirt, shorts and socks, but my usual trainers were not the kind you could run in. Never mind though since my previous pair were not yet too small for me, and they were still somewhere in the garage. I'd go and find them after a quick spot of yoga to loosen me up; I'd be a fool to pull a muscle due to not warming up properly. Having seen bits of Mum's routine, I figured that I knew enough to get myself stretched out and ready for running. Also, it was only just after eight o'clock, so time was on my side. I stifled a yawn and squatted down, made an arch, closed my eyes and stuck my bottom in the air, all the time holding the poses for a good twenty seconds while breathing deeply in and out. As a final stretch, I then found a very comfortable position of lying on my back with my arms stretched out to the sides. This was an easy pose, so I could hold it for much longer, again, eyes closed and taking long breaths. I was in a deeply relaxed state as I imagined myself next to a trickling blue stream below a snow-topped mountain. Butterflies floated softly by on a gentle breeze, and I could hear the most relaxing musical sounds in harmony with the birdsong. I could envisage tender blades of grass tickling the back of my neck before I slowly started to rise off the ground. I was hovering a foot, no two feet in the air with only a perfect, clear blue sky above me. My body rotated around but continued rising away from the earth so that I was facing downwards and could survey all that was below me. A majestic, tall tree was at the limit of my vision, but that was not going to stop me. I willed myself to fly to it and pushed down hard with my left leg onto the thin air below me. Miraculously, this boosted me high into the sky, and I soared up to reach the same height as the mountain! A bald eagle flew next to me as gravity had stopped pulling me back downwards.

"*Squawk*. You're amazing, Neil!" said the eagle. "Imagine entering the high jump on sports day, or in the Olympics for that matter."

"That's a great idea," I replied. "Fleur would be well impressed if I could boost the world record from just over two metres to two thousand metres. Everyone will think I'm a God."

"Wow, Neil! You're incredible!" shouted a tiny Fleur from down, far below me on the ground. She looked lovely in a bright red dress, and she was waving up at me.

"True," continued the eagle. "She may even want to marry you."

"Neil, I want to marry you!" shouted the mini Fleur, spinning around so that the skirt of her dress made a circle. "I love you!"

"This is all great, Sam," I said to the eagle, as Sam was clearly his name, "but shouldn't I achieve some amazing things with this power of flight that only I possess in all humanity?"

"Ah yes," replied Sam, furrowing his brow feathers. "With great power comes great responsibility." With these words, he shot a spider web from between his talons and caught a giant fly, about the size of a fist, which he then pulled into his beak. "Are you hungry, Neil?"

"Oh Sam, you old joker," I retorted. "You know I don't eat flies. We've been pals for years, and have you ever seen me eat a fly? That time when one flew into my mouth when I was seven doesn't count before you bring that up."

"You know I was going to!" chortled Sam. I looked carefully at his beak as he spoke and was entranced by the way it was solid yet could move and morph to make the mouth shapes to pronounce words. Sam was my good friend, and I felt relaxed around him, up here, gliding high above the world with the wind in my hair.

All of a sudden, Sam turned to me, and his friendly face had changed to a somewhat aggressive snarl. He bobbed his feathery head and sang, "I've got you in my sights, there's a plan that I've hatched. You're getting down with me. It's game, set and snatch." With that, Sam shrank down from a full-sized bird into absolutely nothing.

I was flying solo but had now unexpectedly forgotten how to fly. I glanced down at the world below and noticed that it was rising up to meet me at an alarming rate! My stomach rose up into my chest as I plummeted to the ground. Would I be able to grab the tree branches to break my fall on the way through? I thought that was a possibility until the tree jumped out of my way and planted its roots on the other side of the stream. Just as I was about to hit the ground, Sam reappeared next to me and snored. He then opened my mouth with his wings, shrank himself down and climbed into my gaping maw and snored again.

I woke up with a start on my bedroom floor, snorting back another snore.

"I've got you in my sights, there's a plan that I've hatched. You're getting down with me. It's game, set and snatch." The chorus of 'Game, Set and Snatch' by *Durty Dreamz*, Lemony's favourite band, droned through our shared wall as reality swam back to me. That yoga must have been very relaxing as I'd dozed off. However, Lemony never got up early on a Saturday, so how come she was playing music? I sat up and looked over towards the clock radio on my bedside table. 11:46! I hadn't just dozed; I'd been asleep for hours! Damn. The whole morning had gone, and so far, I'd only managed to drink some water and do a few stretches. No problem. There was still probably time to get my run in before lunch, so I hurried down into the garage to locate those running shoes.

I hadn't had a hunt around in there since the Christmas decoration fiasco, so I wasn't sure exactly where my trainers might be. Fitting a car in there would have been impossible with the number of boxes and the amount of other junk that we had accumulated over the years. Garden tools occupied one corner with a barbecue ready for the hot weather. Painting equipment was piled against the far wall, and beyond that were several cardboard boxes; my trainers had to be in one of those. I opened the first one to find only books, so I was about to close it when it struck me that some of these were my childhood treasures that had become a distant memory. *Sparkly Pipsqueak and the Lost Cheese*, *Tinpot Robot* and the naughty *Captain Fartarse* needed to be read again, and the nostalgic feelings came flooding back to me, the pictures recalling a time and a place full of innocence and happiness.

However, I couldn't spend all day reading children's books when there was muscle to tone. There were only two more boxes, so one of them had to contain shoes. The smell of old socks came from the nearest one, and, lo and behold, there were my trainers just under the cardboard flap. I tried them on to make sure they still fit me; they were a little snug, but I'd still be able to pound the pavement without getting blisters. Curiosity prevented me from setting off immediately on my route, curiosity about what was in the final box. A quick look would take no time, and then I'd be able to concentrate on exercise.

More nostalgia washed over me as I peered into the last box to see photo albums. If I could just flick through them for two minutes, then that was hardly going to set me back, was it? The one with the brown, padded cover was what I was searching for as I knew that was where my early photos started. There I was at about two years old in my favourite blue T-shirt and little red shorts, standing next to Lemony in her bright yellow dress. Even when she must have been about five or six years old, her smile for the camera was more of a smirk, and she was standing next to me with her hands folded neatly in front of her rather than holding my hand. I was trying Daddy's beer in another photo, pinned up against our holiday caravan door by enthusiastic dogs in a third. There were the usual naked photos in the bath, running around the garden, eating sand on the beach, having a cuddle and a story with Nanna Peel, rubbing my eyes and looking sleepy with my knitted alien-looking soft toy that was known as Dolly, and many more besides.

Time must have got the better of me as I was only pulled out of my reverie when Dad came into the garage.

"There you are, Neil," he said. "We've been calling you for about ten minutes. It's lunchtime."

"Already?" I questioned. "Why are we eating so early?"

"What do you mean, early?" he continued. "It's half-past one. Looking through the old photos, are you? Did you find the ones of me when I had a chiselled jawline and a six-pack?"

Half-past one! My trip down memory lane had cost me the beginning of the afternoon, but at least I'd found my running shoes; I could head out after lunch.

The high-protein, low-fat meal I'd been hoping for turned out to be chicken nuggets from the freezer, oven chips and baked beans. Perhaps it wasn't ideal, but it had most of the main food groups, so the balance pleased me. I was fairly stuffed afterwards, so I needed at least half an hour in front of the television to let my meal go down, followed by a relaxing sit on the toilet from where I contemplated a spider that was probably big enough to grab Mum's razor and start shaving its legs. It struggled to climb out of the bath but, thankfully, never quite made it to the rim. Finally, at about three o'clock, I was ready to go and set world records, but first, I just wanted to check my distances were correct. Dad was filling in the crossword with a cup of tea in the kitchen, and he knew about this sort of thing. Actually, he was filling in the crossword with a pen while drinking a cup of tea, but you know what I mean.

"Dad, how far do you reckon it is down to the park and back?" I asked.

"Probably about 800 metres at a guess," he replied.

This was a lot less than I had anticipated. "Are you sure? That doesn't seem very much. Only a mile."

"No," he continued, "I meant 400 metres there and the same back. 800 metres in total."

Either Dad was wrong, or I was useless at judging distances. There was no way I could run to the park and back six times to make up my five kilometres. I needed to readjust the plan. Perhaps I could run there and back but stop along the way for the odd press-up or chin-up. That would still be a good work out.

The conditions were perfect as I stepped outside: not too warm but not too cold. The sky was overcast, but rain didn't seem likely, and there was hardly any breeze. I checked my watch and went for it. A full sprint would be silly in long-distance running, so I set off steadily, at more of a shuffle than a run. Turning the first corner, I recognised old Mrs Brady and her Jack Russell terrier ahead of me. She was trundling along with her walking stick in one hand and lead in the other, but she must have been pretty nifty for a woman in her eighties as I wasn't really gaining on her. I hadn't exactly gone very far, but I was a little out of breath, and so I stopped at a patch of grass, the perfect spot for some press-ups. I assumed the position, feeling the tightness in my shoulders. I lowered myself down but began to shake and my middle gave way. It was more of a tummy-down than a press-up. "Come on, Neil. You've got this," I told myself. Returning to the start position, I was about to begin when I felt a wet tickling at the side of my neck. I jerked away and fell to my right to hear the yapping of Mrs Brady's dog beside me.

"Oooh. Looks like you've found a friend," said Mrs Brady, looking down on me. "My Mr Woofles loves children, don't you, Mr Woofles?"

Mr Woofles, however, yapped some more and then started to nibble at my trainers, snarling and barking as if they were the enemy. He crouched and circled me, growling as I got to my feet, backing away. I tried to put myself behind Mrs Brady, but Mr Woofles darted forward and grabbed my shoe in his jaws.

"Aagh! Get him off me. This mongrel is savaging me!" I shouted, trying to shake the hell hound off my foot.

"Naughty Mr Woofles!" scolded Mrs Brady, nudging the beast with her walking stick. "You're scaring the poor little boy."

I didn't protest about being called a little boy as I was barely escaping with my life here. Mr Woofles gave a little mew of sorrow at being told off by his mistress, and I took that as my cue to skedaddle. The adrenaline from my near-death experience propelled me forwards at pace, and I didn't turn back when Mr Woofles started yapping after me again.

Eventually, in a sweat, I arrived at the park and checked my watch. Could it really have taken me six minutes to run 400 metres? I suppose the incident with Mrs Brady must have lasted longer than I thought. The park was the perfect place to work out a bit more, and I was going to start with the monkey bars. Chin-ups were a life skill, useful if you ever found yourself hanging from a precipice, so I thought I'd start with just the ten to loosen up. I approached the apparatus and climbed up the low stepping bars to reach the horizontal ladder. I grasped the first bar and swung out so that my feet were off the ground. Here we go for number one, I thought. But nothing was happening. I hung there for ten seconds, attempting to hoist myself upwards but in vain.

In due course, I dropped to the ground to contemplate what had gone wrong. The grip! That was it. The overhand grip is much harder, so I should start with an underhand grip. There's no shame in admitting you're a beginner.

I climbed back into the starting position and tensed my muscles. Was I rising? It was difficult to tell but, as I dropped to the ground again, I figured that my wrong grip the first time around must have sapped my strength for the second attempt. Curses!

While I was down at the park, I had a quick go on the swings and the roundabout, and that was energetic at least. I was feeling pretty tired after all of this activity and checked the sky again; perhaps it looked more like rain than I had thought, so a return home was wise. I'm sure that even the Olympic greats don't venture out if there's even the slightest chance of drizzle.

Walking provides a good opportunity for reflection, and so I pondered my progress while striding purposefully towards home. I'd almost certainly break into a run soon, but I wanted to go through my programme first, and it would be difficult to concentrate while running. I checked my stomach to see if my abdominal muscles were showing through yet, and it seemed like they were at the top, rock-solid too, unless that was my ribs. I was wary of the street where I'd been attacked by Mr Woofles, and this contemplation made me forget about jogging home some more. By the time it came back to my mind, I was about fifty yards away from my house, so I put on a finishing sprint and was panting as I knocked on the back door.

"Oh. Well done, Neil," exclaimed Mum as she opened the door for me. "You must be exhausted. Come on in and have a rest."

"Thanks, Mum," I replied. At least someone appreciated my efforts.

Lemony was sitting at the kitchen table, swirling a little fork. The dark crumbs on her side plate and the scrumptious odour in the kitchen told me that Mum had indeed made her gooey, dark chocolate cake. Lemony looked at me scornfully, shaking her head mockingly as she put her fork down and left the room.

"I know you're in training, but do you think you need some cake to replace all those lost calories?" enquired Mum.

"I'll have a snake's portion, please," I replied. "Just a slither."

Mum turned around with a small slice of cake on a plate and presented it to me. It wasn't very big, and I had probably burned off close to a thousand calories in the last hour.

"I could probably manage a larger slither than that," I added, darting out my tongue in a snake-like fashion, so she cut me a much bigger piece which I snarfed down in no time. After all, there were three eggs in this cake, and I needed the protein.

A long bath was what I needed after such a tiring day, and then, after a pizza dinner, there was nothing like an action film to match the active day I'd had. Dad and I settled down on the sofa to watch spiderman, and half-way through, he brought in a big bowl of nachos smothered in guacamole, cream cheese and salsa. Double yummy!

At nine o'clock, I headed up to my room and collapsed onto my bed. I was stuffed and knackered. This training day had been intense, but I would have to go back to taking it easy in future.

Chapter 18
The Stakeout

We'd agreed to meet at seven o'clock at Mrs Jackson's house. That was not too late for the parents who were expecting their children to be spending the evening at someone else's house, but not so early that we'd have hours to kill before the big moment.

I was too nervous to eat much dinner, but Mum had kindly made some sandwiches for us all for later. We had to get into the house and set up, and we'd also have to be aware that Walker and Batesy could possibly make an earlier visit to the area just to make sure that everything would go smoothly for them. We couldn't afford to take any chances with messing up the plan by being too visible beforehand.

"Ready, Neil?" called Dad from the bottom of the stairs.

"Coming," I replied.

I came out of my bedroom with a rucksack full of my stuff. Lemony stood outside her room, leaning against the wall with her arms folded. She looked at me.

"Good luck, and don't screw it up," she said, although she didn't use the word 'screw'. She smiled and went back into her room before I had a chance to answer.

Pride swelled in my dad's eyes, and he smiled at me as we fastened our seatbelts and headed off towards Wilberforce's house. This was the biggest, most grown-up adventure I had ever undertaken, and my pulse was already much faster than normal. Looking out of the car window, I could understand why Walker and Batesy had decided on eleven o'clock for their break-in. The evenings were much lighter now, and full dark was only falling at about ten o'clock.

Dad pulled the car up onto the pavement outside Wilberforce's house, and I jumped out to ring the bell. A vague recollection of the first day of the school year washed back over me as Mrs Pudge answered the door. She looked fairly emotional as she called Wilberforce.

"Hello, Mrs Pudge," I said, thrusting out my hand to shake hers. "I'm Neil."

"Hello, Neil," she replied, accepting my handshake. "So, what will you boys be up to this evening?" she asked nervously.

"Oh," I gulped, not having anticipated this question. "We'll be pretending to be witches and zombies and frightening off the bad guys."

"You boys and your video games," she chuckled, waving away my suggestion as if it might not be the truth.

Wilberforce appeared behind her with a small suitcase in his hand. What must have been the dry ice machine and temperature-control containers were in the hall just behind him.

"You will be careful with the ice, won't you, precious?" said Mrs Pudge to Wilberforce. "Remember how easy it is to burn yourself, so don't forget to use the glove. Why do you need it again?"

She turned to me with that question, so I answered.

"We'll probably have some music later, and it'll create the perfect atmosphere. It's so cool that you could bring that along, Wilberforce."

Mrs Pudge beamed with pride that her boy was going to a friend's house.

"Well, have a lovely time, poppet, and don't forget that you can come back if you feel sad later on," she said, blinking rapidly and letting out a sharp breath to avoid tears forming.

Goodbyes were said, and I helped to carry out the machine and containers while Dad waved to Mrs Pudge as he opened the car boot for us.

"It sounds like quite an escapade for you boys," said Dad, looking in the rear-view mirror once we'd got going. "Are you scared?"

"I don't know if scared is the right word, but I am frightened," answered Wilberforce. "I'm just glad I've got Neil and the others to help me."

"Too right," I replied. "Just keep your eyes on the prize. If we do this right, then those two numpties will be off your case for good."

Sounding so brave had surprised me, but I suppose I'd just reminded myself why we were doing this, and my dislike of Walker and Batesy was giving me an adrenaline boost.

We arrived at Mrs Jackson's house on Broomstick Lane just after seven o'clock; Cameron, Stephen and Grub were already there, having arrived all together. Curtains in one of the downstairs windows twitched before they all filed out to help us bring in the equipment. Dad wished us well and then drove off, leaving us to it. The house smelled of unflushed public toilets and false teeth at first, but I was soon used to the staleness, and we couldn't really open any windows if we were supposed to be hiding in an empty house. Stephen seemed to have finished filling Cameron and Grub in on how he'd hated yesterday's cricket match, so he felt no further need to repeat it again for me.

Thankfully, Grub didn't live far away, so they had been able to balance his karaoke system and lights on Cameron's skateboard to drag over. We laid out everything we had brought and looked over it before nodding to each other and going through the roles we each had in every stage of the plan.

Grub, the techie, was in charge of lights and smoke. He tested a lot of different colours on his LED light system before deciding that a bluey-purple was the spookiest colour. That was just a switch to flick, but the dry ice machine required more effort. A masterclass from Wilberforce showed how you had to have a lot of boiling water in the tank, and then you added the dry ice crystals in to create the smoke. You had to wear a glove because solid carbon dioxide was so cold that it could burn skin, but you also had to be careful about how much to add in at a time. Grub was going to be positioned around the corner, in the dining room and out of sight of the front door.

Stephen was going to be similarly tucked out of the way but in the lounge, on the other side of the front door. His role was to get Lemony's yellow contact lenses into Wilberforce's eyes as quickly as possible before opening the front door as if by magic. He would then switch to the microphone on Grub's karaoke system to provide spooky noises, made even deeper by using my Darth Vader voice changer. Grub had already found a backing track that pulsed deep bass sounds, and we just about found the perfect volume so that it would cover any hiss from the dry ice machine but not sound too much like a recording or wake any sleeping neighbours.

Cameron had brought his hooded, black dressing gown and was going to wear it back-to-front so that his face would be covered. The intention would be that I would see him in the corner of my vision skateboarding from the lounge to the dining room and vice versa and make a sweeping gesture as if I were summoning him behind Wilberforce who would be standing in the doorway. This would take some practice because skateboarding blind was not easy, so he had to judge exactly when to stop so as not to crash. He spent at least half an hour rolling from side to side with his eyes closed in order to judge the distance as closely as possible.

My main role was, of course, to be a witch, travelling smoothly down the stairlift dressed in Cameron's long Darth Vader cape and Stephen's glowing-eyed Iron Man mask. I'd had a few tries and realised that wedging my knees into the corners of the lift's seat was the best way to achieve the floating effect. It wasn't comfortable at all, and there were screws sticking into my knees when riding the chair this way around, but I was taking one for the team and doing what I had to for the best effect. A black jumper and black tracksuit bottoms looked less witchy in daylight but should be perfect to complete the illusion at night time. I would also act as the initial coordinator, watching the street outside from an upstairs window so that I could give a countdown to the rest of the team. We didn't want smoke, light and sound as Wilberforce came into the house, but the effect needed to be strong as we opened the door after his transformation.

A lack of a plan B meant that we had one shot at this. Our initial set up and checks had all taken place, and so we sat down quietly to eat the sandwiches my mum had prepared. There was room for four of us at the dining room table, which we'd pushed up against the wall in order to leave Cameron room to skateboard into, and more importantly, out of view. Stephen, however, had opted to sit on the floor with his back up against the wall; he looked deep in concentration. Cameron, himself, sat on the window sill staring out through the edge of the curtains into the street. We still had two more hours until we were due to start, and all we had to do now was wait.

The ticking of a grandfather clock was the overriding sound. I looked at Grub who looked back, swallowed a mouthful and pushed his glasses back up the bridge of his nose, giving me an anxious thumbs up. Tick tock. Wilberforce had already gobbled his sandwiches down and was looking nervously around, not helped by the silence. Tick tock. I glanced over to Cameron who was chewing inaudibly, seemingly unaware that we were there too. Tick tock. I looked over to Stephen who was beckoning for Wilberforce to pull him up to his feet. Tick tock. Wilberforce stood and grabbed hold of Stephen's hands leaning backwards, but he only managed to lift him a foot off the ground before Stephen stopped, a stunned look on his face.

"Shhhh!" he whispered, looking to the side.

We all tensed up and listened intently.

Tick tock tick tock…frrrrrt!

Stephen burst out laughing at his own childish wind gag, his fart now machine-gunning out in tandem with his

144

laughter after the initial ripper had stopped when the startled Wilberforce had dropped him.

"Oh, for God's sake," said Cameron, covering his nose pre-emptively.

"Huh-huh," giggled Grub, relieved that the tension was broken.

"Couldn't you have saved that for later?" I asked. "If hell has a smell, then you've just unleashed it, my friend. That could have been useful."

We laughed and then chatted some more as we cleared away our sandwich wrappers. It was intimidating to be in a house where it was getting darker by the minute, yet we weren't able to switch on the lights. Our eyes were becoming accustomed to the twilight, but I could sense the dread brought on by the knowledge that the darker it got, the closer to eleven o'clock it was getting.

"When should I leave and wait for Walker and Batesy?" asked Wilberforce. "And where do you think I should wait?"

I began to ponder the best solution when Cameron spoke up.

"I think it's best for you to stay here. Once we see them arrive, you can go out of the back door. The back gate opens on to a passage that runs behind the houses on Broomstick Lane and then comes out about four houses down in that direction," said Cameron, pointing out to the left of the house.

We'd agreed on a lockdown of total silence and everybody being in their position from quarter to eleven so that there would be no chance of a shadow or a twitching curtain giving us away in case of an early start by Walker and Batesy. Watches and trainers would be removed too so as not to spoil the ghoulish effect.

It was a group decision to allow the bedroom window where I'd be hiding to be left open by the narrowest of angles so that I could hear the conversation in the street if necessary. Of course, I'd have to be super careful not to shout anything within the house, or that would be heard outside just as easily.

By half-past ten, we'd all been to the toilet several times, but the two chimes of the clock gave the last call on that too, in case the flush could be heard from outside. Grub was filling the kettle to get his hot water ready as this was another thing that could not be left too late. My costume was laid out upstairs, but I brought the Iron-Man mask to my face to wish everybody good luck in the tinny voice just for fun. However, the voice sounded exactly like my own.

"What was that?" asked Grub. "Don't forget to switch it on, Neil."

"It is on," I replied hurriedly, checking the switch but noticing that the eyes weren't alight either. "Did you check the batteries, Stephen?"

"No," he answered. "But I only got it for Christmas this year, and I've hardly used it."

"Oh, great!" I said. "A witch who sounds like me. That's hardly believable."

"All right. Don't blame me," snapped Stephen.

"I'm not saying I'm blaming you," I answered. "But it is your fault."

"Stop it you two," said Grub in an animated whisper. "We've only got ten minutes until lockdown. What's the solution? Has anyone got any other batteries?"

I looked at the battery case inside Iron Man's mouthpiece.

"There are some in my Vader mask, but they're not the same kind."

Just then the Iron Man eyes lit up, glowed and dimmed, glowed and dimmed again.

"It's too late to go and get some more. Cameron. Do you know if there'd be any 'double As' in the house anywhere?" I asked.

He led me into the dark kitchen and opened one of the drawers. We both rooted through the keys, screws, cotton reels, paper clips and keys, hunting desperately for some batteries. Grub came back in with the kettle for another lot of hot water. Eventually, I found one battery, and Cameron held up three. "I don't know if they've got any juice left in them," he whispered. "If not, that fading in and out might be a cool effect if the voice thingy does the same."

The chime of the grandfather clock at quarter to eleven meant that we were on lockdown: everybody into position and silence from hereon in. I scurried back through the kitchen as Cameron slipped into his dressing-gown, saving the hood for the last moment, and took his place. As I made for the stairs, I passed Stephen who was checking the contact lenses for the tenth time. His shadow appeared to take note of me, and I held out my hand for a fist bump before heading upstairs. I could have done without this last-minute hitch, but it was Stephen after all, so there was nothing to forgive.

I tiptoed up the stairs before heading into the bedroom. Warily, I approached the gap I'd left deliberately in the curtains and looked outside. No sign of Batesy or Walker yet. I dropped the four batteries onto the bed and sat down to make a switch. It was really hard to see which way round to insert them in the almost total darkness. I put the first pair in and flicked the switch: nothing. A bead of sweat was forming inside my hairline, and I wiped it away with irritation. Curtain check: coast clear. Time to try the next pair of batteries. I reached down and grabbed for the remaining pair, but the ones I'd removed in the first place had rolled against them, and I couldn't tell whether I was putting the same ones back in again or whether they were new ones. Dammit! We'd been here for four hours, and I was in a panic with a few minutes to go. I fumbled to find the positive and negative ends, put in the third pair and flicked the switch: nothing. It seemed like I would have been better off taking my chances with the first pair after all. But which ones were they? Silver and red Energy Boosters, but there was no light in the house any more. Solution required. The street light outside. I held the six batteries up to the slim shaft of light and could just about make out the wording enough to spot the two Energy Booster batteries. But, holy crap! Walker and Batesy were already in front of the house. They were near the street light, looking around furtively. I dropped the four useless batteries onto the bed and scuttled out onto the landing clutching the remaining two in my fist. Knocking twice on the wall, as was our signal, I whispered down to Stephen.

"It's capering time."

He knocked on the wall twice to acknowledge the signal, and then I left it to the rest of my team as I hurried back into the bedroom, grabbing the mask and standing so that I could see the street below. I heard the faint sound of the back-door closing: Wilberforce was on the move. Placing the batteries in correctly had become easier now, and I managed to get them in and close the case fairly quickly. I flicked the switch: full power! Immediately, I flicked the switch back down again to conserve as much battery power as possible and sidled up to the crack in the curtains to observe the next phase. I was adjusting the cape around my neck and pulling up the hood as Wilberforce waddled into view. They both gave him six swift belly punches. I held my breath in an attempt to hear what they were saying.

"You're late, you tit," ejaculated Walker, before going over the plan again. Wilberforce was to have a look around Mrs Jackson's house to make sure nobody was there before standing guard by the front door while the other two cleaned out her house of silver and other valuables.

"Please don't send me in there to check if the coast is clear. She's a witch," blubbered Wilberforce. He was coming across as terrified, which could have been excellent acting, pretending that he didn't know exactly what was in the house, but was most likely actual anxiety about the whole situation.

"Get in there and shout if anything goes wrong," said Walker, brandishing his penknife and swinging his boot into Wilberforce's flabby arse for good measure before pushing him towards the house.

Hurrying to the top of the stairs again, I whispered "Stand by!" to my friends below. I craned my neck down to see Wilberforce enter the house before dashing back into the bedroom to make sure that Batesy and Walker made no sudden moves. However, in my haste, I stubbed my little toe on the corner of the bed and fell down with a great crash. My nose must have rubbed against the switch in the mask because the Iron Man eyes lit up, and my scream of pain came out in a tinny, high-pitched noise. My initial reaction was that I'd probably just ruined all of our work but then, glancing out of the window, I could see that the bullies were both looking up to my window, and they both looked scared. I reached inside the mask and flicked the power off again, watching the scene below. I hoped that Stephen and Wilberforce had had enough time to get the contact lenses in and that Grub had got his special effects going because Walker was heading for the door. I was just about to bolt for the stairs to give Stephen the signal when Batesy grabbed Walker's arm and tugged him back.

"Let's go, Basher," he whimpered. "You heard that howl. The witch has got him. I told you she wasn't really dead. I wanna go home."

"Don't you pussy out on me now," warned Walker. "Even Lard-Ass had the guts to go in there. It was probably just the pipes squeaking. Now let's go."

He grabbed Batesy by the arm and they started for the house. That was as long as I could wait. It was now or never. Avoiding the bed more deftly this time, I rushed around to the top of the stairs and gave Stephen the thumbs up as I clambered into my stairlift, flicked my mask on and covered my head with the hood.

The sight at the bottom of the stairs was incredible. Grub hadn't cracked under pressure one bit. He was out of my sight, but there was a glowing blanket of bluey-purple smoke across the entire floor. Wilberforce was standing in position, smack bang in the centre of the doorway. Over to Stephen as he pulled the string that he'd attached to the door handle with one hand and raised the volume on the karaoke system with his other. A low bass pulse sounded, and it was my turn now. I reached down for the stairlift controls and pushed the down arrow, wedging myself in as firmly as I could for maximum floaty, yet quite painful, effect. I raised my arms slowly above my head and let out a high-pitched wail as I came into Batesy and Walker's view. On cue, Wilberforce dropped slowly to his knees as I lowered my right arm, as if controlling him. I pointed over to the dining room with my left arm as Cameron took the stage. He gave himself a soft push from the crouched position and then floated across the smoke gradually rising to a standing position and spreading his arms. As he glided across the room, Stephen growled through the Darth Vader voice changer and into the microphone for the karaoke system. The effect was truly awesome.

As Cameron passed by, I could see Walker and Batesy clearly in the bluey-purple glow. They had made it to about two metres from the front door but were both frozen to the spot. Their mouths were agape, and their eyes were wide open. Simultaneously, a dark patch appeared at the crotch of both of their trousers as they wet themselves in fright. Batesy turned instantly and fled, screaming as he did so, but Walker remained. As I looked out of the eye slits underneath my Iron Man eyes, I noticed that the glow was fading and returning, fading and returning again. Were my batteries going to fade before we could get to our *pièce de résistance*? This had all been going far too smoothly, and now I was potentially going to snatch defeat from the jaws of victory!

Chapter 19
The Truth Will Set You Free

My eyes were not glowing at all now, and I was panicked internally yet determined not to let it show. I thrust out my right arm to the waiting Cameron who skateboarded back across behind Wilberforce. As Cameron crossed the doorway, Stephen must have noticed my difficulty with the mask because he took matters into his own hands.

"Look inside yourself, Tracy!" he boomed, as Cameron, coming to a smooth stop mid smoke screen, lifted an arm to point at Walker.

Just at that moment, Walker was distracted by the Cameron figure with the rumbling, Stephen voice. His frightened look was now tinged with confusion as he wrinkled his brow. Wilberforce also slowly returned to the standing position but still kept his gaze downwards. I took advantage of this to cross my hands in front of my face, tapping the outside of the battery pack as hard as I could, and moving as carefully as I could off the stairlift and slowly towards Cameron and Wilberforce. Planting my stubbed toe down, however, really hurt and I'd also built up some severe pins and needles in my legs from having had them wedged so firmly in the corners of the seat. One leg almost gave underneath me and the other one too! I tried to move my arms in a jerky fashion too, as if this were the way all witches walked. As I pulled myself up towards vertical, I glanced at Grub who was smiling at my spasmodic lurching; perhaps he thought that this was a purposeful part of my act. All of a sudden, his smile disappeared, and he held his head in his hands in dread. He gestured frantically to the dry ice machine as if to say that it had run out, which gave us only about thirty more seconds before the smoky layer would disappear, revealing our socks, skateboards and light beams, and ruining the effect.

Miraculously, the batteries in my mask hadn't quite given up the ghost yet, and the glow appeared above my eyes again. I had to take the chance that the voice changer was still operational too. I adopted a low voice in case nothing happened.

"Look inside yourself, Tracy!" I uttered, lifting my arm and pointing at Walker. As my eyes glowed and faded under my hood, so the voice changer flipped in and out of working order. This was not part of the plan, but it sounded pretty scary to me, my sentence wobbling between different pitches. I was now standing between Wilberforce and my Cameron minion. Cameron and I still had our arms extended, and we repeated, "Look inside yourself, Tracy!"

Wilberforce raised his head and opened his eyes. He looked at Walker, and Walker looked back. The effect of the yellow contact lenses on him was dramatic. Walker took a step backwards and Wilberforce raised his arm to point. However, he didn't point at Walker so much as behind him and to the side.

"Look *behind* yourself, Tracy!" he howled.

The plan had been for Wilberforce to join us in the same phrase, but he'd seen something appear behind Walker, and his voice contained genuine terror. Walker's fear of us was temporarily redirected as he glanced behind him. He looked back to see the three of us still pointing at him menacingly, but then he realised what he had glimpsed behind him and turned back to face the hideous vision.

A twisted form was rising from a crooked crouch, juddering and twitching as it rose. It seemed to be a humanoid, but its skin was deathly pale-grey, and its hair was tangled and bushy. Dark, dirty rags covered its flesh, and blood dripped from its considerable fangs. Its eyes were, like Wilberforce's, bright yellow within hollow, dark circles. As it got closer to the door, it too raised a finger towards

Walker and exclaimed, "Look inside yourself, Tracy!" in a hideous shriek.

The dry ice had been escaping outside the house, and, although it was evaporating quickly out there, the odd swirl was adding atmosphere in the front garden too. Walker could take no more.

"Get away from me, you spiteful demon!" he yelled.

Walker grimaced and then grasped the back of his trousers. I guess we'd scared the crap out of him. He'd had enough and burst into tears as he fled the front garden and ran off uncomfortably, out of our sight and all the way home.

Wilberforce sidled behind me and grabbed my arm to hide from the demonic being before us.

"Well, that was fun," said a more familiar voice as the 'Lemony beast' pulled the fangs from out of her mouth and strode inside the house. "Who'd have thought that frightening eleven-year-old boys could be so very entertaining?"

Stephen and Grub poked their heads around from their hiding places before stepping into view.

"I'm twelve, actually," said Stephen, puffing out his chest in an attempt to look impressive.

"Mission accomplished?" questioned Grub.

"Mission very much accomplished," I replied. "I think we got three body secretions out of Walker, only two out of Batesy, but two out of three ain't bad."

"As Meatloaf would say," added Lemony. "That was quite a show you were putting on there. Very impressive, and I'm glad to see my contacts were being so well used. I think I'll take those now if you don't mind."

She held her hand out to Wilberforce who eventually managed to remove them before passing them back to Lemony. His eyes were incredibly red and weeping.

"Good God, man. Are you all right?" she asked.

"I have quite a few allergies," replied Wilberforce. "Perhaps I've got conjunctivitis now."

Cameron took Wilberforce inside to run his eyes under a cold tap as Stephen stepped forwards.

"Thanks for helping us, Lemony," he fawned. "You were great. The icing on the cake."

Lemony gave a little faux curtsey.

"It was a pretty good cake in the first place though. Anyway, how did you know where we were, and that dressing up like that would help?" I asked.

"I do listen occasionally, you know, Neil," she replied. "Broomstick Lane, contact lenses, teaching bullies a lesson, blah blah. You seemed to be on a mission, and I thought you could have done with some back-up."

"Too right," said Grub. "The dry ice evaporated the moment Walker scarpered. He'd have found us out any second."

"By the way," continued Lemony. "Who's Tracy?"

"That's Walker's real first name," I replied. "Cameron used to go to the same primary school as him, and he saw it on the school computer system when he had to wait in the secretary's office one day. He's known as Mark, but Cameron was the only one who knew his real first name was Tracy, and so we wanted to get that in to spook him even more."

"You really did save the day, especially when you called him Tracy too," flattered Stephen, a bit too obviously this time.

"Oh Stevie," said Lemony, stepping towards him. "I'm sure you did a great job too."

She grabbed his face and leant in as if to kiss him. I must have looked horrified as Stephen closed his eyes and offered his mouth, opening his lips in hope of something more than a quick peck. Of course, she turned his head at the last moment and wiped the fake blood from her chin across his cheek, back and forth.

"Well, good night all," offered Lemony before turning around and marching away, offering a condescending little wave over her shoulder. "Don't stay out too late. Your mummies and daddies will worry."

Stephen opened his eyes and reached up to his cheek. He rubbed it and smelled his fingers.

"Bloody hell, Stephen. It's not scratch and sniff," I said.

"That counts! That definitely counts as a kiss," he insisted. "And she said I'd done a good job."

"You really don't know anything about girls, do you?" I laughed.

A light had come on in the house opposite Mrs Jackson's, so we closed the front door again before doing a minimal clean-up, congratulating ourselves over and over again, and going over every detail of the evening's roaring success. Apparently, the howl as I stubbed my toe was terrifying, and my jaunty pins and needles walk was better than most Japanese horror films, according to Grub.

Cameron locked up the house, and we agreed to meet back there at midday the next day. It was Bank Holiday Monday, and so my dad would be off work and able to collect all of the equipment. Cameron Stephen and Grub headed back to Stephen's house, and I walked back to Wilberforce's house with him.

When Mrs Pudge opened the door, it was clear that she hadn't been asleep anyway, probably worrying about her pride and joy. She clutched her dressing gown closed at the bosom in one hand and enveloped her son in the other.

"Wilberforce, dear. Are you all right?"

"He's fine, Mrs Pudge," I answered for him, handing Wilberforce's suitcase to her. "We pretended to be witches and zombies, and beat the baddies, but we thought it might be best if he spent the night at home. Plus, he might need some drops as his eyes are quite sore. See you later, Wilberforce. Good night, Mrs Pudge."

With that, I left before she could ask me any more questions and walked home quickly. Tonight, I had been the frightener, but the streets of a quiet village such as Lower Piercing are pretty scary too after midnight. Mum met me at the door and was relieved to hear that everything had more or less gone to plan. I yawned and gave her a kiss before heading upstairs to clean my teeth, get into my pyjamas and collapse into bed. I was exhausted, but I think I fell asleep with a smile on my face.

Chapter 20
The Beginning of Summer

"I feel as if I've really been on a journey with this," I said to Dad as we pulled into our driveway.

"So do I," he answered, switching off the car engine and feigning annoyance. "To Broomstick Lane, then to Grub's, then to Wilberforce's, and finally back here again. Much more of a journey than I'd planned for."

"You know what I mean," I replied. "And you know I'm really grateful to you and Mum. There aren't many parents who would trust their children to do something like we did yesterday, and I think we've really made a difference, even if it's just to one person."

"It's the little things like that which really do make all the difference," he said as we got out of the car. "Lemony asked me not to say anything to you, but even she said that you'd done a great job."

That was about the biggest surprise I'd had all year.

*

Wilberforce had asked about what we had planned for the rest of the half-term break. We'd answered that we were planning to finish off our Dungeons and Dragons quest, if at all possible, in the few days we had remaining. He'd looked a little downcast, so I asked if he wanted to join us. After all, we had a ready-made character called Geoffrey Pantsniffer primed and ready to fight; it wouldn't matter if he'd missed the first part of the adventure. Wilberforce found the name hilarious and laughed like I'd never heard him laugh before.

He accepted happily, but we decided to make him a little more competitive by altering his statistics and equipment. We changed the venue each day, and Mrs Pudge's delight was clearly visible when we all arrived at Wilberforce's house to play on Friday. She provided the most excellent snacks.

The first day back after half-term was a test. Wilberforce's eyes were still puffy and badly bloodshot, despite the drops that he was taking three times a day, but that turned out to be very helpful. We were almost all seated in the form room when Batesy slipped quietly in at the back. People were still chatting about what they had been doing over the break; Ottilie Plank was saying in a loud voice how it had been delightful to spend the week at her parents' villa in Spain where the orange groves in her orchard were far more fragrant than her desk mate at school. I ignored her and was talking to Stephen behind me. I nodded to Wilberforce who was primed to finish the job. Batesy was nervously putting the contents of his bag into his locker, looking this way and that. He had dark circles under his eyes, as if he hadn't been sleeping properly of late.

Wilberforce slowly stood up from his chair and then rotated around to face Batesy, staring directly at him through his fierce, red eyes. Batesy fumbled the few items in his hands and dropped his school bag. He sidled back towards the classroom door, slowly shaking his head, breathing heavily and fighting back tears. Batesy couldn't take his eyes off Wilberforce, and Wilberforce didn't take his eyes off Batesy either. As soon as he made it through the door, he sprinted down the corridor and out of sight. Apparently, he went straight to the school nurse, Mrs Beever who, having established that he didn't need a wee or a poo, sent him straight home.

There was one more barrier to cross and that was done at the first break time. Our English lesson was about to come to an end when I spotted Walker's face through the glass panel in the door. He was pacing nervously back and forth outside. Thankfully, we were in group discussions, so I was able to signal to Wilberforce while Mrs Deanus was busy with another group, without drawing too much attention.

Ottilie spotted that I was distracted and followed my gaze.

"So, Neil Peel," she sneered, looking between Stephen and me. "Is that another recruit for your sad-act group? You've probably got enough members that you could apply for *Britain's Got Talent* in the sad-act category. You could call yourselves the Sad-Acts."

She looked very pleased with herself until there was a tap on her shoulder.

"Can you not think of any more varied vocabulary in your English lesson, Miss Plank?" asked Mrs Deanus as Ottilie flushed bright red. The bell sounded, and we gathered our things together. Fleur smiled at me, which enraged Ottilie even further.

"What is wrong with you?" she asked Fleur. "Why are you siding with him?"

"Live and let live," replied Fleur coolly. "Neil's being friends with someone who doesn't have many. Spread a little happiness, as the song says."

Ottilie gave a harrumph of frustration before storming away to find Remi Solfer, her best, equally bitter friend. It struck me that being successfully unpleasant was much easier if you were clever; Ottilie would never have anything on my sister. I wasn't sure which song Fleur was referencing, but it was my turn to blush when Fleur smiled at me.

"I'm mates with Wilberforce too," added Stephen, looking hopefully at Fleur.

"Good," she replied amiably before gathering her books together and heading to the lockers.

She was perfection.

I grabbed Stephen, and we headed out towards the playground, stopping just outside the main building. Wilberforce had not had a chance to get twenty feet outside of the main corridor before Walker approached him from behind and put a hand on his shoulder. Wilberforce stopped still and slowly looked down at Walker's hand. He then turned around and stared into Walker's eyes through his own weeping red eyes. He raised his arm to point at Walker.

"Look inside yourself, Tr..." he said before Walker interrupted him, quieting him down with a calming hand gesture and lowering Wilberforce's pointing arm. Grub and Cameron had appeared behind Walker too and stayed out of his field of vision but within earshot.

"Now listen, Lar...er...Wilberforce," began Walker through gritted teeth. He was struggling to meet Wilberforce's gaze. "I don't know what that witch did to you in there, and I don't want to know. I don't know, and I don't want to know. If you've got superpowers now, then don't use them on me...Please. I want you to stay out of my way, do you hear? I'll leave you alone if you leave me alone. I promise to look inside myself, but let's never talk about that night again, and don't call me that name any more. Please."

With that, he offered Wilberforce a hand to shake. Wilberforce looked slowly down at the hand and then stared back up into Walker's eyes. He did not shake the hand.

Walker backed away, still held by Wilberforce's gaze. He bumped into an older boy who swung him around so that he nearly fell over.

"Watch where you're going, you little tosser," called the bigger boy.

Once Walker had scarpered, we congratulated Wilberforce on another stellar performance, pointing out that he seemed to be relishing his power a little too much.

*

The rest of the term went by pretty easily, and it wasn't long before we were looking forward to the long summer holiday. We had almost finished our first year at Titfield School, and Mrs Deanus became very upset on the last day. It might have been about us, her 7D class moving on into year eight, but I think she had her own issues outside the school too, and the staff had been allowed wine at lunchtime that day, so there was that as well.

She tried to give us a farewell speech about how we were all developing into lovely young gentlemen and ladies, at which I almost interrupted her to point out that Ottilie Plank, Remi Solfer and Batesy had quite a way to go yet to reach that accolade. However, I kept silent, and she wished us all the best for the summer. Everybody was starting to cringe now and squirm a little in their seats until she finished with her trademark 'Well done to all of those who have done well' phrase, which she enjoyed very much and used far too often. The bell finally rang for the end of the school year, and there was a swell of cheers throughout the school as everybody tore off their ties and spilt out of classrooms and corridors. Cheery faces were all around as pupils and teachers alike discussed their holiday plans while dispersing away from school and into the summer.

*

It struck me that I hadn't got a summer holiday plan at all. We'd probably be around Lower Piercing for the whole six-and-a-half weeks, maybe visiting Nanna and Grandpa for a weekend. Lemony was now considered old enough to look after me at home so that we didn't need childcare while Mum and Dad were at work. Of course, I'd be spending most of my time with Stephen, Grub, Cameron and Wilberforce anyway, so that suited me fine.

There was also the small matter of my birthday, which was fast approaching. It usually fell in the summer holidays, being in mid-July as it was, so I was particularly young for my year, most of my friends having already turned twelve.

Arriving back at home that afternoon, I flopped onto the sofa with a wide smile on my face. This was the longest possible time until I had to go back to school again, and it was to be relished. I fell asleep almost instantly.

The sound of the back-door closing woke me up an hour and a half later. I rubbed my eyes, stretched and shuffled into the kitchen. Mum and Dad were both there, and they looked particularly cheerful.

"Hey! There he is," exclaimed Dad. "Call your sister down, will you, Neil? We've got an announcement."

What? Mum can't be pregnant, can she? That was my first thought as I jolted back into a fully awake mode and called Lemony down.

"Lemony! Mum and Dad have got an announcement for us," I shouted up the stairs.

Ten seconds later, Lemony stomped down the stairs, looking miserable.

"Do you know whether it's a boy or a girl yet?" she asked. "Isn't that a bit irresponsible, getting pregnant at your age? I suppose we'll have to move house because I am not sharing a room with *him* or a baby."

"Hang on," said Mum, looking hurt. "I'm not that old, and I'm not pregnant either."

"No, dear," interrupted Dad. "We've booked a holiday. We're going in three weeks' time. There was an apartment free in the Majorca resort where Mike and Diana are staying, so we've booked it on a cheap, last-minute deal. It's right next door to theirs."

"Oh yes! That's brilliant," I shouted, hugging Mum and Dad. Going on holiday with Stephen would be the best.

"Pardon me for not leaping for joy," moaned Lemony, "but did you really think I'd be delighted to go on holiday with the ginger prince himself perving all over me? How many bedrooms are there in these apartments too because if you think I'm sharing with Neil, then you've got another thing…"

"Relax, darling," smiled Mum. "They're two bedroomed apartments. We've just been around to see Ella's parents to check if she's free that week, which she is, and to check if her passport is in date, which it is."

"So, Neil can share with Stephen in Mike and Diana's apartment," continued Dad with an expectant grin on his face, "and you and Ella can share the other room in our apartment. Sound good?"

Lemony considered this for a while, her frown gradually disappearing and a smile taking its place.

"Actually, that sounds very good," she said. "Thank you, Daddy. Thank you, Mummy. Does it have a balcony, and how big is the pool? Do you have a map of the resort?"

Lemony's enthusiasm was unprecedented, and Mum and Dad had played a blinder in going out of their way to accommodate her wishes. She was more interested in the precise details of where we would be staying, but I was content in the knowledge that I would be spending time in the sun with some of the most important people in my life. It would be a shame that Grub, Cameron and Wilberforce wouldn't be there, but at least, I'd have Mum, Dad, and Stephen.

And Lemony.

The End